I0681246

The Fox Family

BROTHER FOX

ELIZABETH COLDWELL

ENTWINED PUBLISHING

Brother Fox
ISBN # 978-1-80250-263-3
©Copyright Elizabeth Coldwell 2025
Cover Art by Kelly Martin ©Copyright September 2025
Interior text design by Entwined Publishing
Published by Entice, an Entwined Publishing imprint

This is a work of fiction. All characters, places and events are from the author's imagination and should not be confused with fact. Any resemblance to persons, living or dead, events or places is purely coincidental.

All rights reserved. No part of this book may be used, reproduced, or distributed in any form or by any means, including but not limited to electronic, mechanical, photocopying, recording, or by any information storage and retrieval system, without prior written permission from the publisher. This book and its contents are expressly reserved from use in training artificial intelligence technologies or systems. Furthermore, this work is expressly reserved from the text and data mining exception, in accordance with Directive (EU) 2019/790 of the European Parliament and of the Council.

Applications should be addressed in the first instance, in writing, to Entwined Publishing. Unauthorised or restricted acts in relation to this publication may result in civil proceedings and/or criminal prosecution.

The author and illustrator have asserted their respective rights under the Copyright Designs and Patents Acts 1988 (as amended) to be identified as the author of this book and illustrator of the artwork.

Published in 2025 by Entwined Publishing, United Kingdom.

Entwined Publishing is a division of Totally Entwined Group Limited.

BROTHER FOX

Dedication

For the other two-thirds of the Unholy Trinity

Chapter One

Kyle

My dad died twice. He was killed by a hit-and-run driver a couple of weeks before I was born—at least, that's what my mum told me when I was old enough to ask why I only had one parent, unlike the rest of my friends. And for years, I believed it. She only revealed the real story when she got her cancer diagnosis. She admitted she couldn't keep the secret to herself any longer, and that's how I found out I was actually the son of Charlie Fox, head of the most notorious crime family in North London.

Discovering the truth could have been a profound shock for me, but somehow it didn't change the way I thought about myself. It might be a cliché that the apple never falls far from the tree, but in my case it was true. I'd first got involved with petty crime when I was still at school—mostly shoplifting on the local high street or breaking into cars to steal anything of value—and from there I'd only been sucked deeper. I was never cut out for university, or even for a steady nine-to-five job. Not when I could earn so much more money dealing drugs to the kind of people who wanted a couple of ecstasy tablets to liven up their nights out, or a line of coke for their nice middle-class dinner parties. Sometimes I wondered how long I could keep doing this, whether one day I'd sell a bag of pills to a stranger who turned out to be an undercover cop, but so far, I'd kept out of trouble. I'd always had a pretty good nose for knowing who I could trust. And now I knew I had Fox blood running in my veins, I figured I'd always been destined to become part of the criminal underworld. You can't fight fate, or at least that's what my mum believed.

I still didn't know what compelled me to attend his funeral. Maybe I wanted some kind of closure. Maybe I just wanted to be close to the only family members I still had, even if none of them had the faintest clue who I was. There'd be enough ghoulish hangers-on that afternoon, whether they were the kind who found criminality seductive and exciting, or those who simply wanted to dance on Charlie Fox's grave.

The media scrum at the gates to the cemetery proved my instincts correct. For good or ill, images of the funeral would be all over the internet even before the service was finished.

I pulled up the collar of my coat and kept my head low as I sneaked into the church. I doubted anyone would recognise me, but it was safer not to take any risks, especially with all the cameras being shoved in people's faces as they passed by the gaggle of reporters. The funeral wasn't limited to family members only, judging by the number of people packed into the tiny chapel room. I found the last remaining spot on the end of a row right at the back. The elderly man in the adjoining seat didn't even look up as I sat down. On another occasion, I might have taken a moment to look around and appreciate being in such a historic spot, but I didn't want to do anything that might draw attention to myself.

People shuffled to their feet as music began to play. Frank Sinatra crooning *My Way*. I almost laughed aloud. What else could have summed Charlie Fox's life up so perfectly, yet still been such a cheesy and predictable choice for bringing the coffin into the chapel?

The pallbearers made their way down the aisle, their footsteps slow and steady. I glanced up as they passed me, being careful not to make eye contact with any of them. Three of the men shared the same blond hair and tall, lean build. Grief and loss were etched into their features and the one who held the back of the coffin on my side of the aisle had tears glistening on his cheeks. These had to be Charlie's sons — my half-brothers. A lump rose in my throat. We were connected by blood, yet we couldn't have been further apart. And this was definitely neither the time nor the place to introduce myself to them.

As they set the coffin down at the front of the chapel and took their places in the front row, I began to wonder whether I'd done the right thing coming here. Even though Charlie was my father, I didn't belong among these people. I envied their strong sense of family — the way one of the brothers had his hand on another's shoulder, while the third wrapped his arm around a brassy-looking woman I assumed to be their mother.

The vicar — a short, plump woman with greying curly hair — spoke, but I wasn't listening, still too busy studying the Fox brothers. When everyone around me murmured "Amen," I joined in a beat after everyone else. At least the hymn that followed, *All Things Bright and Beautiful,* was one I remembered from school. Still, I was growing increasingly uncomfortable in the middle of all these strangers, some of whom had to be wondering who I was and what I was doing here. I shook my head, telling myself not to be paranoid. The only person anyone cared about at this moment was in that wooden box with the ornate brass handles next to the altar.

"And now," the vicar said, "I would like to invite Cameron Fox to say a few words about his father."

One of the brothers got up and walked to the front of the room. He pulled a piece of paper out of his coat pocket and took a slow, deep breath.

"What can I say about Dad?" He shook his head, making the effort to keep his voice steady. I admired his strength, knowing how hard it had been not to fall apart completely when I found out how little time my mum had left. "I mean, there's been a lot said about him over the past few days, and most of it I don't think I could repeat in a place like this."

A smattering of soft laughter echoed around the church, and Cameron took a moment to appreciate the assembled congregation. A smile flickered across his face. It didn't lighten the sorrow in his eyes.

"Well, I feel like I'm among friends here, and so I can talk about the Charlie Fox we knew, the man who may have done some bad things in his life, but who was a great father to us and a loving husband to my mum, Lynda."

The brassy woman, wrapped up in a stylish black coat with what I doubted was a real fur trim, raised a handkerchief and dabbed her eyes. The Fox brother sitting at the side of her put his arm around her shoulders and gave her a hug as she leaned into him.

"You know," Cameron went on, "even now, it's so hard to believe Dad's really gone. There's part of me still thinks this is all some cruel practical joke on his part and he's going to come striding in here any minute, asking how the Arsenal got on and who fancies a pint in the Duke of Canklow…"

I couldn't listen to any more of this. Every word Cameron spoke, every in-joke he shared, made me realise that however much Fox blood I might have in me, I was still on the outside looking in.

But that's going to change, I vowed. *I'm a part of this family, for better or worse, and I'm going to make damn sure they know I exist.*

Not here, though. Not now. Wait until the time is right…

I got to my feet, unable to spend a moment longer in the claustrophobic little room that smelled of beeswax and calla lilies, and headed for the door. No one noticed me go, still caught up in whatever outrageous anecdote Cameron Fox was telling about his father.

Head down, I made my way out of the chapel building and towards the main gates. The pack of journalists had disappeared, and only a few visitors milled around, some clutching flowers to lay at a grave, others taking selfies on their phones. A stall stood on the forecourt, selling hot drinks and cakes. The enticing aroma of freshly brewed coffee wafted on the wind, reminding me how long it had been since breakfast.

Unable to resist, I wandered over to the stall. It had the kitsch name of Highgate Grounds and a middle-aged woman in a white Arran sweater serving behind the counter.

"Hello there, what can I get you?" she asked.

I studied the chalkboard with the list of drinks written on it. "I'll have a flat white, please. Oh, and I'll take that brownie, too." I gestured to the lone cake

11

sitting on a plate in the display case at the front of the stall, and she slipped it into a paper bag.

"You're lucky, it's the last one I have," the stallholder said. "A bunch of journalists polished off the rest of my stock while they were waiting for the funeral cortege to arrive. Apparently, they're burying some famous gangster—someone mentioned his name, but I'd never heard of him."

I gave a noncommittal grunt in reply, not wanting her to know my connection to the deceased. While I waited for my coffee to brew, I took a bite of the brownie. Rich and studded with chunks of dark chocolate, it almost had me moaning aloud as I savoured it.

"That'll be five pounds fifty," the stallholder told me, setting a paper cup in front of me. "We're card only. I hope that's not a problem?"

"Not at all," I assured her, even though I'd always preferred the anonymity of cash. I reached into my wallet and fished out the pre-paid debit card I used whenever I didn't want my bank to know where I'd been or what I'd been spending money on. I tapped it against the little square card reader and waited for the transaction to go through. "By the way, I have to say this is probably the best brownie I think I've ever eaten."

The stallholder smiled. "Oh, well, you can thank Millie for that." She called over to a red-haired woman who was stowing some boxes in the front pod of a solid-looking cargo bike. "Hey, Millie, there's a gentleman here who loves your cakes."

When Millie turned around, my breath caught in my throat. She had the cutest spattering of freckles across her nose and green eyes that seemed to see deep into my soul. I shook my head and told myself not to be so overly dramatic, even if she was the most attractive woman I'd seen in a long time. I'd always had a thing about redheads, and this one ticked all my boxes.

"So, I have a fan?" She had a strong Manchester accent and a hint of laughter in her voice. *I could listen to her speak all day. She'd even sound sexy if she was telling me to take the bins out.*

With a smile, I held up the half-eaten brownie. "Guilty as charged. But this is delicious, honestly. Now I know how good the snacks here are, I'll have to visit on a regular basis."

I half-expected her to turn away then, bringing the conversation to a swift halt, but instead, she seemed more than happy to keep talking to me. Maybe she didn't hear many compliments from the customers who bought her cakes. "So, were you on a guided tour, or…visiting a particular grave?"

I took another sip of my coffee, appreciating Millie's sensitivity. "No, I was here for my father's funeral."

"Oh." Her expression shuttered for a moment. She must know who I'd been here to mourn, and she didn't seem to like it. The darkness left her eyes as swiftly as it had arrived. "I'm sorry for your loss."

"Thank you." Whatever I'd expected her to say, it hadn't been that. "I can probably guess what you're thinking, me being related to someone like Charlie Fox, but to be honest, we weren't that close. In fact, I only discovered we were related a few weeks ago."

"That must have been hard for you…finding him and then losing him again so soon."

So soon I'd never even had the chance to meet him, let alone get to know him at all, but I didn't need to tell Millie that.

Her gaze met mine, and she patted my forearm in a gesture of sympathy. My body tingled at the slight

13

contact, responding in the most unexpected of ways, and boldness gripped me. We'd made a connection—I was sure I wasn't deluding myself about the way she looked at me, or the strength of my reaction to her touch—and I was anxious to spend more time in her company. "Look, I hope this doesn't sound too forward, but I was thinking… After the day I've had, I could do with something a little stronger than this coffee, good though it is. Would you like to come for a drink with me?"

"Oh, I'd love to, but…" Millie glanced at her bike. "I really need to drop everything off at home." I must have done a pretty bad job at hiding my disappointment because she went on, "Why don't you come over to mine? I have a nice bottle of merlot in the wine rack that a client sent me as a thank-you. Maybe I could open that and we could talk?"

"You know, that sounds just what I need right now."

"Okay, well, let me give you my details so you can meet me there." When I didn't reply immediately, wondering why she didn't want us to travel to her place together, she added, "I mean, you will be driving over, won't you? And I'm on my bike, so…"

"Sure, of course." I snapped back to the moment, dismissing any thought that she might not want to be seen leaving the cemetery with the illegitimate son of a crime boss. I handed her my phone and she typed her address and phone number into my contacts list. "I gave you the postcode so you can put it in your satnav."

I glanced at the details she'd given me and shook my head. "No, I think I know where you are. Just off Rosebery Avenue, right? I make a couple of regular deliveries round Myddelton Square, so I know the area pretty well."

Millie fished a cycling helmet out of the bike pod and started buckling it in place. "Well, I'll catch you there…"

It took me a moment to realise I hadn't given her my name. "Kyle."

"And I'm Millie." She flushed, even the tip of her nose turning a pretty shade of red. Somehow, being flustered only made her more adorable. "Oh, but Sheila on the stall told you that already, didn't she?" She patted her pockets and fished out the lock to her bike chain. "Anyway, I'll see you shortly."

"Can't wait," I murmured, but she'd clambered onto her bike and was already heading for the cemetery gates.

She lived a good four miles from here, and I tried to work out how long it would take her to cycle home. I didn't doubt it would take me less time to get there, avoiding the worst of the early evening traffic by taking a shortcut through the back streets of Camden.

Behind me, a car door opened and slammed shut, and I wondered whether people were beginning to leave Charlie Fox's funeral. Not wanting to be caught hanging around, I dashed over to where I'd parked up.

As I put the key in the ignition, Millie's cute, freckled face swam in my vision. The thought of her kind heart and that oh so arousing accent kept me smiling all the way to the heart of Clerkenwell.

Chapter Two

Kyle

Millie's directions took me to an imposing redbrick building at the end of a quiet, tree-lined street. With its white stuccoed frontage and big windows, it looked more like a civic suite of offices than a block of apartments, and I checked again that I'd come to the right address. Could baking cakes really be so lucrative that she could afford to live in a place like this? A couple of bikes were slotted into a rack in front of the building, but they were the ones you can rent by the hour to get you around London, in the bright-red livery of the bank who sponsored their use. I had no clue as to where Millie might leave hers, or if she'd even arrived.

It didn't surprise me to see the uniformed concierge on the door. It explained why Millie had been happy to invite a man she'd never met before back to her home. Not that I meant her any harm, but she had the security of at least one person in this swanky apartment block knowing she'd had a visitor, if anything bad should happen.

He looked me up and down, making me feel glad that I was dressed in something smarter than my usual jeans and puffer jacket. "Good afternoon, sir."

"Hi. I'm here to see Millie…" I realised with a start I didn't know her surname. "She lives in apartment seven. Is she back yet?"

Whatever the concierge was about to say was drowned out by Millie's cheerful shout. "Kyle! You found it okay." She took off her helmet and shook out her hair as she dashed into the lobby. "Hey, George, how are you this afternoon?"

The concierge dipped his head in a discreet nod. "Nice to see you, Miss Jeffers."

Millie hooked her arm in mine. "Come on up, and I'll give you the grand tour."

She led me into a wide hall with an arched glass roof, and we headed for a bank of lifts at the far end.

I swivelled my head to the left then the right, taking in the elegant surroundings. A door was flung open and a young man in sweatpants and a sleeveless vest emerged, giving me a glimpse into a gym with state-of-the-art workout equipment. "This place is fantastic," I commented.

"I know. I was so lucky to find it before property prices in the area went completely through the roof. It used to be the headquarters of one of the main utility companies until they moved out in the late nineties, and that's when it was converted into flats."

She called the lift, and a moment later, the doors slid open. I followed her in and watched as she pressed the button for the top floor. We travelled up in silence. I had so many questions to ask, but I didn't quite know where to start. The lads I drank with in my local would have taken one look at Millie and laughed at how far out of my league she was, but somehow, I felt comfortable in her company, as if I'd known her much longer than I had.

The lift glided to a halt, and we got out. Downstairs, there'd been a faint smell of beeswax and lemon floor polish. Here, a pot of white and purple orchids scented the air, and our feet sank into the thick blue carpet as we walked down the hallway. Everything screamed understated luxury, and I wondered what kind of people Millie's neighbours were. Not the kind who took advantage of the service I provided, that was for sure, otherwise I'd have found myself paying a visit to this beautiful building long before now.

Millie unlocked the door to one of the apartments and led me inside. Without being asked, I slipped my shoes off and left them in the hall with my overcoat. My mum had brought me up to know that it was the polite thing to do. Her words rang in my head. *Kyle, not everyone wants dirt and mess tracking into their carpets.* Millie had parquet flooring, polished to a shine and easy enough to keep clean, but still, Mum had always taught me good manners cost nothing.

"Take a seat in the living room, and I'll be through in a minute with the wine," Millie said before disappearing in what I assumed to be the direction of the kitchen.

I made myself comfortable on the black leather chesterfield and took a discreet look around while Millie fetched our drinks. Soft grey walls, a geometric-patterned rug on the floor, and a couple of pieces of abstract art, all blue and green swirls of paint. Nothing personal, no family photos or knick-knacks. I got up and went over to examine the bookshelf by one of the large windows, hoping that would give me a little more insight into what Millie was like as a person, when she returned carrying a tray. On it was a bottle of wine and two long-stemmed glasses, and a bowl filled with mixed nuts.

"Interesting painting," I commented, for lack of something else to say, nodding to the far wall.

"You like it? My friend Amanda painted it. It's her tribute to the Impressionists."

I nodded, not wanting to admit to her that I didn't really know who or what an Impressionist was, and went back to where I'd been sitting.

"Yes," Millie went on, taking a seat next to me, "that was her present to me on my last birthday. She wanted to give me something she knew no one else would have, you know?"

"Well, it's certainly more original than an Amazon gift voucher." I smiled as she put the tray down on the coffee table in front of us and reached for the corkscrew. "But tell me about how you got into selling brownies."

She fixed me with a sceptical expression. "You really want to know?"

"I buy and sell things myself. Import-export, that kind of thing." It was the same vague wording I used whenever anyone showed an interest in what I might do for a living. "Have you been doing it long?"

"A little over a year. I used to work for one of the big financial services companies in the City. The pay was amazing, and I made some really good friends there, like Amanda. But we were under an incredible amount of pressure to deliver results, and most of the time I found myself working sixty- or seventy-hour weeks. And there's only so long you can put up with that kind of stress before you crack. So, when they announced they would be downsizing the department and were looking for people to take voluntary redundancy, mine was the first name on the list."

I nodded. It explained how she'd had the money to buy a place like this, but I still had questions. "Okay, but how do you go from working with money all day to baking brownies? Not to be rude or anything, but it doesn't seem like a natural career progression."

She pulled the cork out of the bottle with an audible pop. "There's that awful cliché that if you do a job you love then you'll never work a day in your life. Hand me one of those wine glasses, would you, Kyle? Thanks." As she poured the wine, she continued, "And I've always loved to bake. My best memories of my mum are the ones where the two of us are in the big old kitchen in the house where I grew up, and she's getting me to stir cake batter or whisk egg whites for a lemon meringue pie. I can still smell the warm scent of sugar and vanilla that used to fill the room..." She took a long sip of her wine, her eyes misty with a faraway expression. "Anyway, she taught me everything I know about cooking, and the pay-off from my City job was big enough that I didn't have to worry about covering the bills for a while, so I thought, why not give this a try?"

I drank from my own glass. I'd never really been into wine, preferring a bottle of lager or the German Weissbier they had on tap in my local pub, but I liked how this merlot tasted, rich and fruity on my tongue.

"I tested my recipes on the people I used to work with, wanting to know what they thought, and which ones would sell best. They got used to me turning up at the office once a week with a batch of something sweet for their coffee break. Salted caramel brownies or blondies with cranberries and pistachios or – "

"Blondies?" I cut in, a vision of my mum's small but cherished record collection flashing into my mind. "Like the band?"

Millie laughed. "No, they're a similar type of traybake to a brownie, but you add white chocolate to them instead of dark, so they come out pale and interesting but still delicious."

There was an obvious comment about Debbie Harry to be made, but I bit it back. I didn't want Millie to think I had the same sexist views of women as my dad had spouted at length—at least according to what my mum had told me about him. Instead, I helped myself to a handful of nuts.

"Anyway, I'd been doing my research, and I knew that letterbox brownies was the way to go." She must have seen my bafflement because she laughed. "Yeah, they are a thing, Kyle. Go on a site like Etsy, and you'll see loads of people selling sweet treats online. Presents you can have posted on your behalf and personalise when it's someone's birthday or wedding. So that's what I did at first, taking orders and sending them out once a week." She paused and took a long sip of her wine, a thoughtful expression in her eyes. "But getting asked to supply the cakes for the stall at Highgate really made the difference. Having that regular order means the business is now at the point where it's viable for me to take on an assistant to help out with the baking and packaging up the orders for delivery. The next step would be to open physical premises of my own—I mean, that's the dream, but finding the right place is going to be hard, especially as rents anywhere in Central and the nicer parts of North London are so expensive."

It wasn't a problem I'd ever had to deal with, but I could appreciate why she might struggle. Even the biggest redundancy pay-off wouldn't last forever.

Almost without my being aware of it, we'd shifted closer together on the couch. When she reached for the wine bottle to pour us both a refill, her thigh brushed against mine, sending a powerful charge through me.

"Only a small one for me," I cautioned her, trying to push away the thoughts that rose in my mind of how those thighs of hers would feel wrapped around the small of my back as we fucked. "I'm driving."

"Oh, of course." Again, that cute flush appeared on her cheeks as she tipped wine into her own glass.

I'd broken so many other laws during my lifetime, but the one thing I would never do was run the risk of being pulled over for a breath test. Not only could I lose my licence if I was over the limit but my details would also be in the system from then on, and I really didn't want the police to have any information on me if I could possibly help it.

"But what about you?" Millie asked, breaking the silence that had settled between us. "I mean, I invited you here in case you wanted to talk about what you were going through, and all I've done is prattle on about cakes."

"Hey, that's fine. Sitting here with you, drinking nice wine, it's been just what I needed. Yeah, this afternoon was a little rough, sitting in that church, looking over at the family I should have been a part of..." I let out a heavy sigh. "But it is what it is. Maybe things would have been different if my dad had been in my life when I was a kid, but I'll never know. And my mum did a pretty great job of bringing me up on her own, so I'm grateful for that."

"So, you're close to your mother?"

"I am, though she's not too well at the moment."

And doesn't stand a chance of getting any better, according to the doctor treating her in the hospice. I didn't add the last bit, simply drank the dregs of my wine. Millie didn't need to be burdened with my woes.

"Oh, I'm sorry to hear that." She pressed her body even closer to mine. She had an uncertain look on her face, as if she wanted to hug me but didn't know whether it would be crossing a line. All I wanted to do was kiss that uncertainty away. Our eyes met, and before I knew what I was doing, my lips were on hers.

Millie didn't pull away. Instead, she wrapped her arm around the back of my neck as the kiss deepened. She tasted of the wine we'd been drinking and a delicious sweetness that was all her own, and she sighed into my mouth. Time faded for a moment as I gave in to the urge I'd been fighting since that first press of her firm body against mine.

I put my hand on her leg, high up on her thigh, and she broke the kiss. My first instinct was to apologise, since I was sure I'd gone too far. "Millie, I'm sorry, I should have asked if you wanted me to do that."

"No, it's okay. I...I just don't want to feel like I'm taking advantage of you."

You? Take advantage of me? I almost laughed at the thought, but she was serious.

"I mean," she went on, "you buried your dad today, and you just told me your mum's ill, and here I am —"

"Please," I cut in before she could beat herself up any more, "don't worry about it. What happened just now, it was exactly what I needed. And I'd like to do it again. Maybe not tonight, if you're not comfortable with that, but soon. Hey, maybe I could take you out for dinner? I know this great little Vietnamese place hidden away down a back street. It's a bit basic but the food is out of this world."

"Sounds nice." Millie's face brightened.

"Okay." I pulled out my phone and scrolled to my calendar. "So, how does next Tuesday at seven sound?"

Millie nodded.

"Right, I'll see you then." I got to my feet. I was desperate to linger but the notifications that had piled up on the screen of my phone while I'd been here reminded me I had places to be. Places it was safer Millie never knew about. "Thanks for everything."

I gave her one last hug, like I wanted to commit the feel of her and the scent of her perfume to my memory, then I was out of the door and heading for the lifts.

I made sure to wish George the concierge goodnight. I had the feeling, if things progressed with Millie the way I hoped they would, he'd be seeing me come in and out of this building on a regular basis.

Chapter Three

Millie

I sat in the living room for a long while after Kyle left, finishing off the last of the wine in the bottle and wondering why I hadn't asked him to stay. More importantly, I mused on the fact that he hadn't made any effort to convince me otherwise when I'd told him I thought he was in a vulnerable place, given everything that had happened to him today. Maybe, I told myself, it proved my instincts about him were right. He was a nice guy who'd discovered he was related to some bad people, and like anyone would in those circumstances, he'd found himself questioning a few things.

With a sigh, I drained my drink, stood to take the empty glasses to the kitchen, then sat back down. What I wanted most right now was to talk to someone who could help me sort out my scrambled thoughts. On impulse, I reached for my phone and scrolled to the list of contacts. Right at the top was Amanda's name, and I didn't hesitate to dial her number. If anyone could give me the advice I needed, it was her.

She picked up on the third ring. "Hey, girl! How are ya?"

I couldn't help smiling at the sound of her cheerful Texan drawl, blunted only a little by her years in London. In the background, I heard the chatter of voices, and I glanced at the clock, wondering if she was still at her desk. Company policy was strictly no personal calls unless it was the direst emergency, and I didn't think my current emotional dilemma fell into that category.

"Oh, are you still at work? I can call you later if you are."

"No, that's fine. I just got out of the office, and I'm picking up a few things for dinner for Jim and me."

"Anything nice?" For as long as I'd known her, Amanda had been on some health kick or another. The last time we'd been out for a meal together, she'd been cutting carbs out of her diet, and I wondered if that was still the case.

"Oh, some salmon fillets, egg noodles, a little pak choi…"

My stomach growled as she reeled off her shopping list. I'd barely picked at the nuts I'd brought out for Kyle and me, and now my body was telling me I ought to eat. "Sounds delicious. You'll have to give me the recipe."

"Yeah, it's this whole pescatarian thing I'm trying. I read this article that said eating oily fish is fantastic for your brain and it makes your skin softer, so I thought, what the hell? And I'd got so fed up with never eating bread. I mean, if the good Lord had wanted us to avoid carbs, he wouldn't have made sourdough toast taste so good, right? Anyway, what's going on with you,

Millie? I'm sorry I haven't been in touch a whole heap recently, but work's been so hectic the last couple weeks, you know, what with those new tax rules in the Budget and the big clamour for AI stocks, and—"

"Well, partly I wanted to catch up with you, but mostly I needed some advice. You see, I met this guy today."

"Really? Tell me all about—oh, what do you mean, unexpected item in bagging area?" Amanda let out an exasperated huff and I tried not to smile at the thought of her doing battle with the supermarket's self-service checkout machine. "Sorry about that, Millie... No, I'm not paying by gift card, you stupid... Oh, there we go. Anyway, who is he, and where did you meet him?"

"His name's Kyle, and he was at the cemetery today for a funeral. He liked my brownies, we got talking, and somehow, I invited him back to my place. We had a couple of drinks, we kissed, then—"

"Hey, should this wait till I get back home?" Amanda said with a laugh. "You know, in case things are about to get X-rated."

"That's what I wanted to talk to you about. Nothing happened, apart from the kiss. I mean, Kyle had just buried his dad, and it didn't seem like the right time to be taking things to the bedroom."

"But you sound like you wanted to."

"Yes, I did, and you know I'm not the kind of person who usually has sex on the first date. And this wasn't even a date. But there was a...spark, you know. Something I don't think I've ever felt with anyone else—at least, not as sudden as this."

"So, what's he like? Don't tell me—one of those blond, kinda nerdy guys you always fall for."

I closed my eyes, picturing him in my mind. "No, he's...different. He's tall, dark-haired. A bit rough around the edges."

"A bad boy? Be careful, Millie. Those are the worst." Amanda always liked to think she was looking out for me. It was one of the things I cherished about her.

"Well, I'm not sure about that, but I do know his dad was a local gangster."

"Seriously? Like the Kray twins?" A tone of awe entered her voice, as if I'd somehow found myself involved with royalty.

"Kyle didn't tell me the details, but when the funeral procession arrived and a whole load of journalists turned up, I got the impression he was some sort of a big deal in the area."

"So, you didn't do anything more than kiss...what did you say his name was? Kyle?"

"That's right."

"Mm. And was he a good kisser?"

I couldn't prevent a small smile from quirking my lips. "You could say that."

"All right, way to go, Kyle. And are you seeing him again?"

"He's invited me out to dinner next week."

"Well, I am going to want all the sordid details...so there'd better be some sordid details, do you hear me?" Amanda's words were punctuated by the rustle of plastic bags and the clicking of a key turning in a lock. "Hey, honey, I'm home," she called out before turning her attention back to me. "Okay, I expect to hear from you when you've been on that date but if you want to speak to me before then, I'll be around."

A thought occurred to me. "Didn't you say this was the weekend you and Jim were going to that B&B in the Cotswolds?"

"Shoot, you're right. But still, if you need me, call me. It might go to voicemail if we're making the most of the bed part of bed and breakfast, but…"

"Goodnight, Amanda."

I set down the phone, happy to have caught up with Amanda, even if our conversation had left some of my questions unanswered.

My thoughts strayed back to Kyle, the softness of his lips and the feel of his strong body pressed against my own as we'd kissed. A pleasant shiver went through me at the memory. It was far too long since anyone had kissed me with so much passion, so much pure, undisguised need, and I cursed myself again for putting a stop to things when I had.

Sitting around thinking about what could have been wouldn't get me any closer to the next time I saw Kyle. As I reached over to grab the wine glasses we'd used, the muscles in my shoulder twinged and I let out a soft groan.

A long soak in a hot bath would soothe the aches and pains that came from cycling around the city and spending most of the day on my feet. I dumped the glasses in the kitchen sink, then went to fill the tub. As the water streamed from the taps, I threw in a couple of handfuls of lavender-scented Epsom salts. From experience, I knew that inhaling the scented steam would lead to a good night's sleep, leaving me refreshed for a busy morning of fulfilling the latest batch of orders for my letterbox brownies.

When I began to undress, I couldn't help imagining it was Kyle's capable hands with their lightly calloused fingertips pulling my sweater over my head, then easing down my camouflage-patterned leggings. I yearned to feel him touching and stroking the skin he uncovered with the removal of each garment and pressing his lips to the side of my neck and running them the length of my collarbone.

Caught up in the fantasy I was weaving, I stripped off my underwear, twisted my hair into a topknot that I secured with an elastic band, and slipped into the bath. With my eyes closed, all I could picture was Kyle standing by the side of the tub, shrugging off his suit jacket before turning his attention to the buttons of his crisp white shirt.

"I'm going to make you feel so good," he growled, letting the shirt drop to the bathroom floor. The sight of his hard, muscular torso with a sprinkle of dark hair across his pecs had me letting out a wanton moan. I dropped a hand down between my legs, so I could touch myself there, but Kyle snapped, "Hey, none of that until I say you can."

It didn't surprise me that the Kyle of my imagination had a dominant streak. Whenever I played with myself, I was always guaranteed to come hard and fast if I dreamed up a scenario where I was required to submit. And everything I'd learned about Kyle in the short time we'd spent together made it easy to picture him telling me what to do. I didn't subscribe to the theory that he was a bad boy, as Amanda had claimed, simply because he was related to a man who'd been part of the criminal underworld, but he certainly had an aura unlike any guy I'd dated before. It wasn't too hard to believe he might get off on pulling the strings, and I leaned my head back against the firm white bath pillow and returned to the thought of him undressing while I watched.

He disposed of his trousers without ceremony, but took his time peeling down his underwear, giving me just enough of a peek at the dark bush surrounding his dick to have me desperate to see more. The grey boxer-briefs he wore showed off the contours of his cock, already more than half erect as he at last tugged down the clinging jersey material.

I bit my lip at the sight of him displayed in all his glory, hard and ready for me. I wanted to reach out and stroke my fingers down his impressive length, but I knew Kyle called the shots in this situation and I wouldn't be allowed to touch him without his permission.

"Please, may I...sir?" The word came so naturally to me, without Kyle having to prompt me, and his lips curved in a knowing smile. He didn't say anything. He simply gave a curt nod as he walked closer to the edge of the tub and allowed me to stretch out a hand and wrap my fingers around him.

He was warm and thick in my grasp, a gentle pulse beating in time with his heart, and I stroked up and down his shaft a couple of times.

"You're going to look so beautiful with your lips wrapped around it," he murmured, and I didn't contradict him. If he told me to get down on my knees on the bathroom floor then and there and suck him until he came, I would do it. I licked my lips in anticipation of how he would taste, clean and salty on my tongue.

Kyle helped me out of the bath and draped a towel around me. He dried me off, then urged me down to the floor, until my face was level with his jutting cock. As I moved to take him between my lips, he grasped tight hold of my messy topknot. With my hair clutched in his fist, he could control the speed and depth of my movements, taking control of this blow job.

I shuddered, lost in the fantasy of being willingly helpless in the face of Kyle's whims and made to satisfy his needs ahead of my own. Heat built in my core, and I spread my legs a little wider, but I didn't touch myself, as badly as I wanted to. That could wait till I was snuggled into my soft terrycloth robe and lying on my bed. Maybe I would even dig my vibrator out of my bedside drawer and slide it deep into my pussy, imagining it was Kyle who was fucking me as I did.

Unable to resist any longer, I heaved myself out of the bath and shrugged on my robe. With it belted securely around my waist, I padded through to the bedroom and threw myself down on the bed. There was a bottle of lube in the nightstand along with my bullet-style vibrator, and I drizzled a generous amount over the head of the soft silicon toy before lying back and easing it inside me. It wasn't as long or as thick as I imagined Kyle's dick to be, but when I turned the base and it hummed into life, I didn't care. Delicious tremors rippled through me, and I moved the vibrator up through its speed settings before settling on the one that was always guaranteed to have me coming within moments.

Breathing in shallow pants and throwing my head back against the covers, I pictured myself sucking hard on Kyle's cock as he ordered me to bring myself off with my fingers.

"That's it." He was fighting hard to keep his voice steady, but I could tell just how close he was to spilling his load down my throat. I glanced up to see him with his eyes tight shut and his body braced as he fought the losing battle not to come. *"That's it, take it all...oh, you're such a good girl."*

I pulled the little bullet out of me and ran its buzzing head over and around my clit. The battery-powered stimulation, exactly where I needed it the most, was all I needed to take me over the edge. My pussy muscles clenched hard and I cried out Kyle's name, wishing more than anything he was there to take me in his arms and hold me.

"You'll see him on Tuesday night," I told myself as I put away the vibrator and went to make myself an omelette. In that moment, Tuesday seemed like a lifetime away.

Chapter Four

Kyle

"Cheers, mate." I handed the taxi driver a ten-pound note and told him to keep the change. I would have driven to the hospice, but the street parking in this part of Hackney was limited to non-existent, and what few visitor spots were available in the hospice carpark were reserved for the families of end-of-life care patients. At least, I consoled myself as I made my way to the reception area, Mum didn't fall into that category yet, though, from what the doctor treating her had told me on my last visit, it wouldn't be too long before she did.

As always, I took a moment to compose myself before I went inside. I never wanted Mum to see me looking anything less than relaxed and cheerful, no matter what might be going on in my life. She had enough to worry about, and I didn't want to add to her concern. In truth, thoughts of Millie and our date tonight should have had a smile glued to my face. Every night as I'd been falling asleep, the memory of our kiss had drifted into my mind—her petite body enveloped in my arms, the fresh, summery scent of whatever perfume she wore. But I couldn't shake the nagging sense of resentment that clouded the way we'd met, the reason I'd been at the cemetery in the first place. I needed to know whether my mum had been viewed as Charlie Fox's dirty little secret, and that's why she'd kept knowledge of his relationship to me hidden away for all these years. And how much did the rest of the Fox family know about me? As far as I was concerned, they owed me an explanation, and I was growing increasingly determined to extract one from them by whatever means necessary.

I scrubbed a hand across my face. This wasn't the time or place to start planning my campaign to get answers from the Foxes. Mum was expecting to see me, and right now, nothing else mattered but making the most of however much time we had left together.

I'd been coming here long enough that I knew almost all the front-facing staff by name, but I didn't recognise the girl on reception. I guessed she must be one of the volunteers who helped to keep the hospice running, so I sauntered up to the desk and flashed her my most winning smile.

"Hi, I'm Kyle Ferguson. I'm here to see Joanna on Our Lady ward."

"Of course, Kyle. If I could ask you to sanitise your hands before you go through." She gestured to a large bottle of antibacterial hand gel on the reception desk. "And as I'm sure you know," she continued as I squeezed a dollop of the medicinal-smelling gel into my palm, "face masks for visitors aren't compulsory but if you want to wear one, I have some here…"

I shook my head. "That won't be necessary." When Mum had first been admitted to the auspices of St Susan's, I'd used my charm to wangle her a bed in a single room, knowing she would appreciate the little bit of privacy it offered her. "Thanks, anyway."

I made my way up to Our Lady ward. As I climbed the stairs, I had a view through the large windows down onto the lawn behind the main building, where a group of elderly people sat in wheelchairs, enjoying the unseasonably warm day. I might not hold with the religious beliefs that underpinned the work of the hospice, but I couldn't deny the quality of the care it offered. And Mum had been most insistent that she came here now she had grown too weak to look after herself.

Again, I regretted that she hadn't told me about her diagnosis earlier. I could have helped make things more comfortable for her, paid for her to get private medical treatment, ensured she had the best of everything. But she'd always liked to do things her own way, rather than rely on me — or anyone else, for that matter.

Mum's room was at the end of a short corridor smelling of antiseptic and pine floor cleaner. I took a breath, plastered a smile on my face and pushed open the door. She was propped up against the pillows watching the TV, where a woman I vaguely recognised from one of the soap operas was talking about the latest styles of jeans. Mum had a bright, multi-coloured scarf wrapped around her head and her lips were painted in the shade of pale coral she'd always worn. Her pale face brightened a little as I walked in.

"Kyle, how are you, sweetheart?" She reached for the remote and muted the sound on the television.

"Hey, Mum." I bent and pressed a kiss to her cheek. Her skin was like tissue paper beneath my lips, stretched too tightly across the angles of her cheekbones, and I tried to ignore how the shadows beneath her eyes seemed darker and deeper than the last time I'd seen her. I took a seat by the side of the bed. "I got you some flowers." As I spoke, I brought out the bouquet of crimson roses – Mum's favourite – that I'd been holding behind my back.

"Oh, those are lovely." Mum took a sniff of their fragrance. "You do spoil me. Put them over there where I can see them." She gestured to a small table in the corner of the sparsely furnished room. I took the wilting bouquet of flowers from the vase that stood on the table and tossed them in the wastebin before arranging the roses in their place. Then I dragged a chair over to the side of the bed and took a seat.

"So, are you feeling all right today?" I asked, the ritual question that began every one of our conversations these days. I tried not to think about the reason she was in here, the tumour in her stomach that had gone undiscovered until it was too late to do anything about it.

"Not too bad, love. Though I've got this ache all the way across my shoulders…"

She didn't need to say anything else. "Okay, then, let's make you more comfortable." I rose and rearranged the pillows she was propped against. "That better?"

With a weak nod, she mouthed, "Thank you."

"Have you had any other visitors since I was here last?"

"Well, your Auntie Cheryl popped in a couple of days ago. She was the one who brought those chrysanthemums."

Cheryl wasn't any kind of blood relation, just one of my mother's oldest friends, but I'd always been encouraged to call her 'Auntie' when I was a kid, and the name stuck even now.

"We had a good chat," she went on. "She and your Uncle Brian are off to their villa in Roquetas at the end of the week, so I don't know when I'll see her next. But she was asking after you, Kyle. She said…" Mum broke into one of the increasingly frequent coughing fits she suffered from. When she spoke again, her voice was faint. "Could I have some water, please, love?"

"Sure." I poured a little from the jug by her bed into a plastic beaker and held it to her lips. She took a few sips then motioned to me to take the beaker away. I turned my head for a moment, not wanting her to be aware of how much her obvious discomfort distressed me. Mum had always been the strongest, most independent woman I knew, and now, to see her as this frail shadow of her former self threatened to bring tears to my eyes.

"So…" Mum reached out a bony hand and I took it in mine. "Do you have any news for me? Been up to anything nice?"

I couldn't help the smile that came to my lips. "Actually, I'm taking a woman out to dinner tonight."

"Really?" Mum did her best to sit up a little straighter in bed, fixing me with her beady, intent gaze. "Who is she? Anyone I know?"

I shook my head. "Her name's Millie. She has this business where she sells cakes, and I met her when I was at Highgate cemetery the other day."

"You went to Highgate?" Mum's voice was ice-cold, and I immediately sensed I'd said the wrong thing. "You were at Charlie Fox's funeral, weren't you?" She shook her head. "Oh, you stupid..." I didn't know whether she was referring to me or to herself. "I knew I shouldn't have said anything to you. I should have known you wouldn't be able to keep away from that vicious lot."

"But I had to." All at once, I was the little boy Mum had told off for breaking the twirling ballerina figure in the music box where she kept her jewellery, simply because I hadn't been able to resist creeping into her bedroom and playing with it when she was out of the house. She had a look that could worm any confession out of me, a look that instantly had me feeling guilty. But I wasn't that boy any longer, and I wasn't sorry for what I'd done. "Don't you understand? All these years, you led me to think my dad was dead, and then when I find out who he really was, you just expect me to — what, file the information away and get on with my life?" I fought to keep my voice level, not wanting the sounds of our argument to disturb whoever might be in the neighbouring room.

"Kyle, love, nothing good ever came from being involved with Charlie Fox." She must have realised how those words sounded to me because she hastily added, "Apart from you, of course. You're the one part of me and Charlie being together that I will never regret. But whatever you think you'll achieve by raking things up after all this time, I promise you, you're not going to like what you find."

"I'm sorry, but I have to do this, Mum. I have to go and see...what's her name, Lynda Fox?"

Mum was about to speak, but her words gave way to more coughing, her body shaking under the stark white sheets. I helped her to sip more water, waiting till she'd composed herself. "I didn't want to tell you this, but I suppose there's no use keeping it from you any longer. I'm sure if you speak to Lynda" — the way she spoke her name made it sound like poison in her mouth — "she'll make me sound like some conniving little bitch who sunk my hooks into her man, but it wasn't like that at all."

"Then tell me how it was. I need to understand."

She sighed and rested her head back against the pillow, like the memory was too painful to recall. At last, she turned her face to me. "Charlie Fox was the only man I ever really loved. I was nineteen when I met him, and waiting tables in this little Italian restaurant in Clerkenwell. He used to come in at least once a week — I didn't realise it was because he was collecting money from Silvio, the owner of the place, as part of some kind of protection racket. I just found him funny and handsome and not like any other man I'd ever met."

She looked at me, her expression faraway, as if she was reliving those days all over again.

"So, what...? He swept you off your feet?"

"Pretty much. He had this — I don't know — dangerous aura about him, I guess is the only way I can describe it. And I was attracted to him. We'd chat, but I didn't have a clue that he was married, or that he had a young family, and when he started flirting with me, well, this might sound like something out of a bad romance novel, but I was helpless to resist."

Millie's cute, freckled features appeared without prompting in my mind, and I gave Mum's hand a little squeeze, knowing what she meant. "It's okay. I can understand, honestly."

"One night, he was the last customer in the place, sitting drinking with Silvio while we were tidying up around him. Silvio asked me to get them both a glass of mirto — that's this liqueur the Italians make from myrtle berries — and Charlie said I should have one too. I mean, I barely drank in those days, and I told him I couldn't because I was working, but Charlie insisted. I can still taste it now, so strong, like fire burning all the way down to my stomach, but in a good way. We were laughing about it, and our eyes met..." Mum bit her lip at the memory. "Well, when we'd cashed out the tips and I was about to leave for the night, Charlie said it would make sense for him to make sure I got home safe... And that was the first time I slept with him."

I shifted in my seat, hoping Mum was going to spare me the more intimate details of her affair with Charlie Fox.

She seemed to sense my discomfort because she hurried on. "After that night, Charlie kept coming back for more, and I never turned him down. I'd been seeing him for about a month when I was walking down St John Street one afternoon on my way to work and I noticed him on the other side of the road with this blonde woman hanging off his arm and a little boy who looked so much like him..."

Her voice broke, and I reached for the beaker in case she needed more water, but she shook her head, her mouth set in a grim line.

"The next time I saw Charlie, I confronted him about what I'd seen, and he tried to weasel out of it, telling me I must have been mistaken. But I wasn't going to take that kind of nonsense from him, and eventually he admitted he was married, but he swore he was going to leave his wife for me. He was just waiting for the right moment to tell her about us. And then...then I started feeling sick in the mornings and I realised how long it had been since I'd last had my period. I took a pregnancy test, it showed up positive straight away, and that's when Charlie dumped me."

Her matter-of fact tone took me aback, though it shouldn't have surprised me that someone who would happily cheat on his wife wouldn't treat the other woman in his life any better.

"Not long after that, Charlie was arrested for robbing a security van, and after he went to prison, I never saw him again." She let out a faint sigh. "And you wonder why I don't want you to have anything to do with that family."

"I'm sorry for what happened to you, Mum. But I still need to do this."

Whatever she said wasn't going to change my mind, but she didn't have the opportunity. The door swung open and Marcia, the constantly cheerful West Indian nurse who often stepped in to check on Mum, entered the room.

"Good afternoon, Joanna. Nice to see you again, Kyle." She turned her beaming smile on each of us in turn, then went to check on the machine that monitored Mum's vital signs. "Looking good," she said with an approving nod.

I made a discreet check of my phone screen and winced as I registered the time. My visits to the hospice always seemed to fly by far too fast. And much as I wanted to stay a little longer, I had an appointment to keep in Haggerston.

"Sorry, Mum, I'm going to have to love you and leave you." I kissed her cheek again. "I've got to go and see a man about a van."

"Come back soon." She did her best to smile, but I could tell something pained her, and I hoped Marcia was going to check on Mum's morphine levels before she left. Then she caught my hand and hissed in my ear, "And stay away from those Foxes, do you hear me?"

I slipped out of the room without a reply. However much she begged me not to track them down, I knew I had to speak to Charlie's wife and my half-brothers. We were bonded by blood, even if they didn't know it yet, and I was determined to find out all I could about the father I had never known.

Chapter Five

Millie

"This is the Mildmay Line to Stratford. The next stop is Hackney Central." At the sound of the recorded announcement, I stuffed the book I'd been reading back into my bag, hoisted it over my shoulder and got to my feet. A couple of other passengers shuffled down the aisle past me and I joined them in queueing to get off the Overground train.

I'd been surprised when Kyle said he'd meet me at the station. I'd expected him to pick me up from my apartment, but the train journey had given me time to daydream about what he might have planned for the evening. He'd mentioned a Vietnamese restaurant, but I couldn't help wondering about what might come after that.

When I came down the steps from the platform and emerged onto the busy street, Kyle waited for me, leaning against the wall by a coffee kiosk that was closed for the night. He pulled his wireless headphones out of his ears and came to sweep me up in a powerful one-armed hug.

"Hi, Millie. Looking good." His smile creased the fine skin around his eyes and the kiss he pressed to my lips, not caring whether anyone passing by was watching us, had me melting.

"Have you been waiting long?"

He shook his head. "A couple of minutes. I must have been on the train that came in just before yours."

"So, you didn't think of driving here?" I asked as he started to walk down the street at a leisurely pace, and I fell into step beside him.

"Not if I'm intending on drinking tonight. There's no way I'd do anything to risk losing my licence. I'd be screwed without it. And anyway, there's barely anywhere to park around here, unless you're a resident. That's why I..." He seemed about to add something, then changed his mind.

"Why you?" I prodded, wondering what had caused him to clam up.

He sighed. "You know I told you my mum is ill? Well, she's receiving palliative care in St Susan's hospice down the road from here."

"Oh, Kyle. I'm sorry." I could tell what he'd left unspoken. Whatever was wrong with his mother, she wasn't going to recover. Though he sounded like he'd come to terms with the situation, I didn't want to say the wrong thing and risk upsetting him.

"Hey, it's okay. She's getting the best treatment they can offer, and the staff there are great. But it means I'm pretty familiar with this area by now. Actually, I popped in for a visit there earlier today, and I ended up telling her all about you."

"All good, I hope," I said with a grin.

"Of course. I think she was keen to make sure there'll be someone keeping me on the straight and narrow after she's gone…" His tone was cheerful, but a sudden darkness clouded his eyes, as if the joke had cut too close to the bone.

Amanda's voice floated back to me. *A bad boy? Be careful, Millie. Those are the worst.* But I didn't have any proof Kyle was anything other than what he appeared to be—some kind of small-time wheeler and dealer who was close to his mother and who was grappling with the fact that she wouldn't be around much longer. I had no idea what it was like to have a gaping hole in your life where your dad should have been, or to have missed out on that relationship growing up, and I had no idea how it might have affected Kyle.

I didn't get the chance to respond to what he'd said, because he went on, "Before we go for dinner, we need to nip in here."

I looked to where he'd come to a halt and realised that we were standing outside a small convenience store. Plastic bowls of various fruit and vegetables stood on a low table supported plastic crates, and a sign over the door announced *English, Turkish, Polish and African foods*.

Kyle pushed open the door and I followed him in, past shelves and chiller cabinets piled high with everything from basmati rice to coils of smoked sausage. He went to a refrigerated unit at the back of the store and took out a bottle of prosecco. The bored-looking lad on the counter stopped scrolling on his phone long enough to wrap it in a twist of white tissue paper and ring up the purchase on the cash register.

"The place we're going doesn't take reservations, and it doesn't have a licence to sell liquor," Kyle explained as we left the shop, "but you can bring your own booze." He shrugged. "I told you it was basic…"

"Honestly, it doesn't make any difference to me," I assured him. "I'm always up for trying something new."

He smirked as we turned the corner, heading for the series of railway arches beneath the Overground line. "I'm filing that information away for future reference."

How does he manage to twist everything I say, to make it sound so filthy? Not that I cared. I recalled the fantasy I'd weaved about Kyle the night we'd met—and a couple of equally naughty ones I'd enjoyed since then—and knew I'd be happy to experiment with him, in and out of bed.

We passed a unit where you could get your car serviced and a small brewery tap room, its doors open to the night air and the rhythmic beat of techno music coming from within, and reached the arch at the end of the row. *Tinh Vi* was written in bright-red letters above the door, and when we went inside, we found ourselves in a small room with an open kitchen at one end and seven or eight small wooden tables filling the available space. LED candles flickered on every table, something sizzled in a wok, giving off an appetising savoury aroma, and overhead, I heard the dull, rhythmic rumble of a train passing by on the tracks.

A Vietnamese girl who looked barely out of her teens came over to us, clutching a stack of A4 sheets with the menu printed on them.

"Table for two, please," Kyle said.

"Come this way." Her accent was pure East London. She weaved her way through the already occupied tables and led us to the last remaining spot, close to the kitchen. She placed a menu down on each of the place settings. "I'll be back right away to take your order."

"Great. But before you go, could you open this for us, please?" Kyle unwrapped the bottle we'd brought and handed it to her. She put it on the table, walked off and returned a moment later with two champagne flutes. As Kyle and I took our seats, she deftly uncorked the bottle and poured us each a glass.

I raised an eyebrow as the waitress went to deal with a couple at the neighbouring table who wanted to pay their bill. "Couldn't you have done that yourself?"

"They charge corkage, so it's all part of the service." He raised his glass. "Anyway, here's to a pleasant evening — and new experiences."

Again, he gave the phrase a clear double meaning, and I shivered as a thrill of expectation ran through me.

I sipped my drink, enjoying how the bubbles fizzed on my tongue.

"You know, for something from a corner shop, this isn't half bad," Kyle commented.

"I thought you weren't a wine drinker?"

"I'm not, but Mum likes a glass of fizz at Christmas. I can tell when something's barely a step up from vinegar and this — this I'd drink again. Particularly if the company was the same…"

"Are you ready to order?" The waitress's voice startled me. She hadn't been joking when she'd said she'd be back straight away. I hadn't even had time to look at the menu. I glanced at Kyle, hoping he'd ask for a couple of minutes longer to make our decision.

"You okay if I order for both of us?" he asked me.

I nodded, trusting that he wouldn't pick anything with ridiculous levels of chilli heat. I didn't mind a certain level of spice in my food, but I hated anything that left my tastebuds numb after a few mouthfuls.

Kyle offered the waitress his most charming smile. I couldn't help noticing how her expression softened in response, and she giggled as she held her pen poised over her notepad. "Okay, we'll have the summer rolls and the vegetable dumplings as a starter, and we'll be sharing those. Then we'll each have the pho." He pronounced the word with confidence. "The seafood special for me and...the rare beef for Millie. That'll be all, thanks." When she'd gone to deliver our order to the chef, he told me, "I chose you their speciality – if you're coming here, it makes sense to have what they do best. Plus, I just wanted to prove I know it's 'fuh', not 'foe'. Made a complete fool of myself the first time I came here and asked for that..."

I reckoned anyone who reacted to Kyle the way the waitress had would be pretty forgiving of his mistakes.

"I'm sure, however you say it, if everything here tastes as good as it smells, I'm not going to be disappointed." I smiled at him. "You know, it's funny, when I was working in the City, my boss at the firm used to love to take us all out to celebrate when he landed a contract with an important client. We went to so many different restaurants thanks to him, but somehow, I've never eaten Vietnamese."

"Are you sure you don't miss working there?" Kyle asked.

My answer was interrupted by the arrival of the waitress with our starters. She placed the plates of summer rolls and dumplings down in the middle of the table, along with a little white bowl containing some kind of dipping sauce.

"After you..." Kyle waited for me to help myself.

I took one of the translucent rolls, filled with what looked like prawns, lettuce and beansprouts. To my surprise, it was cold. I dipped one end into the sauce and took a bite.

"I'm not sure what I was expecting, but this is delicious. The sauce has a real tang to it."

"That's probably due to the fish sauce," Kyle said, helping himself to a dumpling. "Anyway, you were telling me about the place you used to work…"

"I was, and no, I don't miss the firm, but I miss the people sometimes. I told you our boss used to take us out for food, but the place he really loved was this karaoke bar in Soho that had private rooms you could hire by the hour. And once you've seen your line manager get up on a table and belt out *I Believe in a Thing Called Love*, you get a whole new respect for him."

"Sounds like fun. When you work for yourself, you don't really get to do much in the way of team building."

"And you've always been self-employed?"

"Pretty much." He took a long swig of his prosecco and topped up his glass, then mine, even though I'd hardly touched my own drink. "I guess I never liked the thought of making a load of money for somebody else when I could be making it for myself."

Our starter plates were empty, and the waitress took them away.

"I get what you mean." I twirled the stem of my champagne flute between my fingers, lost in thought for a moment. "But I liked the security of a nine-to-five job, even if my hours were more like seven to seven. Plus, when you work for yourself, you miss out on things like paid holidays and sick leave."

"Swings and roundabouts," Kyle murmured, as the waitress arrived with two steaming bowls containing our noodles. My mouth watered at the savoury aroma as she set mine before me.

Kyle watched as I spooned up some of the broth, in which paper-thin slices of beef, vegetables, sprigs of coriander and slices of chilli floated. When I tasted it, I didn't speak for a moment, relishing the rich, umami flavour.

"Good?" he said, as I let out a little moan of appreciation.

I nodded. "But is it okay if I don't eat these bits of chilli?"

"Oh, you're a spicy food wimp?" Kyle grinned at me. "Maybe I should have taken you for a cheese toastie instead."

"Hey, don't knock cheese toasties. There's this guy has a stall at Borough Market makes them on sourdough bread with three kinds of cheese and caramelised onions — you have never tasted anything so good in your life..."

"Well, maybe you can treat me to one of those next time."

"So, there's going to be a next time, is there? You sound pretty confident about that." I loved the way our conversation flowed. The light, bantering tone between us made me feel like I'd known Kyle forever, and warmth rippled through me at the thought that he wanted to see me again. Amanda would have told me to slow down, not to give my heart away too fast, but I recalled all the guys she'd tried to set me up with over the years, and how disastrously those dates had gone, and decided to trust my own instincts this time.

"You can't tell me you're not having fun. Okay, so we're not up on the table singing karaoke, but even so…"

The rest of the meal flew by, and almost before I knew it, we'd drunk the last of the prosecco and Kyle had asked the waitress for the bill. This wasn't the kind of place where you lingered over coffee after you'd finished eating, and my heart sank at the thought that our date might be over already.

The night air was chilly after the warmth of the busy restaurant, and I shivered. Kyle must have noticed because he pulled me to him and gave me a hug.

"It's far too early to say goodnight, and I was going to suggest we walk down the road and find somewhere to get a nightcap, but I can see you're cold, so why don't you come back to mine? I make a mean Irish coffee…"

I nodded. "I'd like that."

We walked back past the other arches, Kyle keeping his arm wrapped around me the whole way. I leaned into his side, enjoying the warmth of his body. As we turned the corner onto Mare Street, a black cab came into view, its yellow *For Hire* sign lit up.

"Hey, our luck's in." Kyle waved an arm to flag the cab down. It pulled to a halt beside us. Kyle opened the door and ushered me inside. I couldn't help feeling that so long as I was with him, I would always be lucky.

Chapter Six

Kyle

As the driver pulled away from the kerb, I gave him my address. Millie snuggled up against me on the back seat and we settled back to enjoy the ride.

"You both had a nice evening?" the driver asked in a gruff, nicotine-laced voice, glancing between us and his rear-view mirror.

"Very nice, thank you," Millie replied, in a tone that I could tell conveyed she was trying to be polite but didn't really want to make small talk. The cabbie must have picked up on it because he turned up the football commentary and started listening to that instead.

If I'd been in the cab on my own, I was sure I'd have ended up in a conversation about how badly West Ham were doing this season, and how their manager was bound to get the sack if results didn't pick up soon, but as it was, I had Millie in my arms, warm and soft and with her hair smelling of jasmine. Not caring that the driver might see, I took the point of her chin between my fingers and kissed her.

Her lips parted, and the kiss grew deeper. I put my hand on her knee, just below the hem of her dress, and moved my fingertips in slow, gentle circles. She didn't object as I moved a little higher, stroking her thigh. When she laced her fingers in my hair and pulled my mouth harder on to hers, I knew she was into what I was doing, so I let my hand rest on the soft swell of her pussy, cupping it with my palm.

Millie stiffened at my touch. I broke the kiss to ask, "Are you okay with this?"

If she told me to slow down or stop, I'd do it, but she murmured in my ear, "Keep doing that. It feels so nice."

Satisfied she was just as much into this as I was, I went back to stroking her through her underwear, smiling to myself at how damp the fabric felt.

When the cab came to a halt at a set of traffic lights and didn't move away as soon as they changed to green, earning an angry blast of the horn from the vehicle behind us, I began to suspect that the driver wasn't paying as much attention to the radio as I'd thought. I glanced up and, out of the corner of my eye, I caught him looking our way, a little smirk on his doughy, unshaven face. His eyes met mine in the mirror and he gave me a nod of approval. Millie's skirt was rucked up around the tops of her thighs and I guessed he'd caught a glimpse of her lacy pink panties.

As much as Millie was responding to my kisses and touches, I doubted she'd be happy to learn she was giving our cabbie a free show. There were other girls I'd been with who I wouldn't have thought twice about playing with while a stranger looked on, but Millie... Already I knew she was something special, a cut above the women I'd dated in the past, and I wanted her to be mine alone.

I pulled my hand away, earning a little whimper of disappointment from her. When she looked at me, clearly about to tell me not to stop what I was doing, I jerked my head in the direction of the driver. She must have realised he'd been watching us and getting off on it because she settled back in her seat and pulled her skirt down.

Minutes later, we turned into the street where I lived.

"If you could just pull up behind that black SUV..." I instructed the cabbie.

"Of course, mate." He brought the cab to a halt in the residents' bay across from the main entrance to the block of flats and I helped Millie get out before paying him.

When he tried to give me my change, I waved his hand away.

He smiled at my generosity. It was a ridiculous tip for the length of the journey, but I hoped it would make up for his disappointment at not getting a sexy performance from Millie and me. "Thanks a lot, mate. Have a good night."

Oh, I intend to, I wanted to tell him, but instead I ushered Millie across the street and keyed in the six-number code to open the main door.

We took the lift to the top floor. As soon as the doors slid open and let us in, I was kissing Millie again, unable to keep my hands off her.

"I want you so much," I growled in her ear, pushing her up against the mirrored wall of the lift. Her only reply was a drawn-out moan that had me getting even harder in my jeans. I wanted to rip her clothes off and plunge my cock into her, but that would have to wait until we were safely inside my flat.

Millie wrapped her hands around the back of my neck, pushing her body against mine, grinding on my already hardening dick. For a moment I thought about the CCTV in the lift, then decided I didn't care. I was sure no one ever checked it anyway.

We staggered out of the lift and down the hallway to my front door, pausing every few seconds to kiss again. I fumbled with my key and let us inside.

The door had barely closed behind us before Millie had me pressed up against the wall in the narrow hall and was kissing me with a hunger that took my breath away. She hadn't been lying when she said she wanted me, and I was ready to give her whatever she asked for.

She plucked at my jacket, pulling it from my shoulders, and between us we got it off. I let it drop to the floor, not caring where it fell, then turned my attention to Millie's dress. It fastened with a belt around her waist, and when I pulled that open, the two halves of the dress came apart. Beneath it, she had on a bra in the same shade of pink as her panties, and I ran my tongue across my parched lips at the sight. I didn't know whether she'd worn a matching set because she thought she'd be treating me to the sight of it later, or whether her underwear came as cute and lacy as standard. All I knew was she looked gorgeous in it, and I couldn't wait to strip it off her.

While she fumbled with my belt buckle, I pulled the cups of the bra down, letting her pert breasts fall free of them. Already, her nipples were stiff pink points, and I bent my head and took one of them between my lips.

Millie's breath was harsh and urgent in my ear as I sucked on her tits and ran my tongue over each swollen nipple in turn. She smelled so good, and the feel of her cool fingers as she reached into my open fly and took my cock in her grasp made my head swim.

A couple of strokes of her hand up and down my length had me fully erect and aching to push myself inside her, but this wasn't the time to get carried away. I needed to check Millie was happy with how fast things were moving.

I raised my head and looked her in the eye. Already, her gaze was unfocused, shining with lust. I didn't doubt that she wanted me as much as I wanted her, but still I growled, "I want to fuck you. Is that okay?"

She smiled at me, sweeping aside the soft waves of hair that had tumbled into her face. "More than okay. I mean, I'd be lying if I said I usually slept with a man on the first date, but you... I just can't resist you, Kyle."

Her words were like an electrical charge straight to my dick. It surged up, harder than before, and when she stroked her thumb over the head, smearing drops of pre-cum around the sensitive tip, I almost lost it.

Fighting to regain control, I grabbed hold of her panties and tugged them. They slithered down to her ankles, and she kicked her feet free of them. I peeked at her crotch, liking what I saw. She'd trimmed the fluffy red hair there into a neat little triangle, and for a moment I thought about dropping to my knees so I could eat her out. Already, I could imagine the soft little gasps she'd make and the way she'd pull my head harder onto her as I licked and nibbled her clit. But there was plenty of time for that later. All I wanted right now was to sink my cock into her.

I had condoms in my jeans pocket. I'd shoved them in there before I left to meet Millie tonight, not really thinking I'd need to use them but wanting to be prepared whatever happened. Mum had always drilled the importance of safe sex into me, maybe because of what had happened between her and Charlie. The irony was that if she'd been more careful then, I wouldn't be around for her to lecture me on taking precautions. Still, I pulled the little foil packet out and handed it to Millie so she could tear it open. Between us, we skinned the latex down over my hard cock.

With her back against the wall, I hoisted her into position, taking hold of her soft, bare arse cheeks and lifting her up. She grabbed onto my shoulders as I lined myself up with the entrance to her pussy, then slid into her with one long, determined thrust. She cried out, and for a moment I thought I might have gone too far, too fast, but she simply whispered, "Sorry, it's been a while since I had anything quite so big inside me."

I had to fight not to break into a self-satisfied smirk at her confession. I held myself steady, not moving, simply relishing the sensation of being buried in her hot, wet channel. "If you want me to take it slowly, I will."

"Maybe 'til I get used to you…"

"Okay." I kissed my way along the side of her neck, barely thrusting at first. She gripped me like a velvet glove, and I didn't think I'd ever felt anything so good. She relaxed in my arms, and when I broke off from nuzzling her skin to stare into her eyes, she gave me a little smile and traced her fingertip over my lips before pushing it between them. I took that as a signal to pick up the pace, starting to fuck her with real intensity.

Sweat beaded on my shoulders and slid down my back, and the hallway filled with the musky scent of our lovemaking. We barely broke eye contact, as if we couldn't bear to disrupt the connection between us, stronger than anything I'd ever experienced. If this was the only night we had — and I hoped with all my heart that wouldn't be the case — then I knew it would be one that I'd remember for the rest of my life.

Feeling the cum beginning to surge in my tight balls, I stepped things up a gear. Each stroke pushed her against the wall, and she clung tight to me, her arms around my neck and her ankles locked together at the small of my back as I banged her with everything I possessed.

"Yes, yes, yes," she gasped, the word a mantra she repeated over and over. "That's it, Kyle. Keep doing that. I'm so close. So close…"

She tightened around me and cried out my name as she came, and that was all it took to trigger my own orgasm.

I held her for a long moment before I eased my cock out of her and helped her to a standing position. I couldn't help noticing her legs trembled a little as I set her down.

"Thank you," she murmured.

I reached to remove the condom. "Let me just dispose of this, and then I'll get you that nightcap."

She arched her brow. "Nightcap? I thought that was what we just did. I know I'll sleep well after it."

I grinned and pulled her into a hug, feeling drowsy myself but happy to stand there and enjoy her delicious scent and feel her heart beating against mine. Somehow, being here with her felt right, and I didn't want to do anything that might spoil what we had between us in this moment.

Chapter Seven

Millie

When I woke, it took me a few moments to work out where I was. I didn't recognise the steel-blue bedcovers I was snuggled in, or the neat and tidy bedroom with its plain white walls and floor-skimming blackout curtains at the window. Gradually, memories of the night before came back to me. Kyle, fucking me hard and fast while he held me up against the wall in his hallway, then the gentle kisses and caresses as we'd drifted off to sleep together in this big bed.

The covers at the side of me were pushed back, and there was no sign of Kyle. I had no idea how long I'd slept, and my phone was in my bag in the living room, so I couldn't check the time. The smell of coffee wafted into the bedroom through the partly open door. What I assumed to be Kyle's burgundy and grey striped bathrobe hung on a hook on the back of the door, and I got out of bed so I could grab it and wrap it around my naked body.

Barefoot, I walked through the flat in search of Kyle. I found him in the kitchen, dressed in dark sweatpants and a grey polo shirt and standing in front of a sleek bean-to-cup coffee machine, mug in hand. The time display on the built-in oven let me know it was already gone half-past-eight.

"Good morning," I murmured, smoothing locks of my hair behind my ears.

"Hey, sleepyhead." Kyle smiled at me as I walked closer. "What can I get you to drink? Black coffee? Latte? Cappuccino?"

"A latte would be amazing, thanks. Though I hadn't realised it was quite so late." Worry creased my forehead as I thought about all the things I needed to do today.

Kyle set about pressing the touchscreen on the front of the machine and the kitchen echoed to the sound of coffee beans being ground. "Well, we had a pretty intense night, and when I got up, I didn't want to wake you. But isn't that the beauty of being your own boss? You don't have to clock in for work on time if you don't want to. And anyway, I wouldn't exactly call sleeping 'til eight-thirty a long lie-in."

"Maybe not, but I have a batch of brownies to deliver to Sheila at Highgate Grounds, and if I let her down, she might decide to get her cakes from somebody more reliable in future."

"It's okay. When you've finished your coffee, I'll drive you back to your place. And I'll give you a hand with whatever needs to be done."

I smiled, genuinely grateful for Kyle's offer of help. "But don't you have to work today?"

He shook his head and handed me my latte. "Not until later this afternoon. So, if you want me to help you with boxing up cakes or whatever, I'll gladly do it."

"Thanks."

We went into the living room. Kyle flopped down on the couch. I took my cup of coffee over to the window and looked out over the tops of the surrounding buildings. Last night, I'd been too wrapped up in him to pay much attention to the place where he lived, but now I was keen to find out more.

The roof of the Olympic Stadium was a looming silhouette against the cloudy sky. "I didn't realise you were so close to the Olympic Park here," I commented.

"Yeah, it's very handy if I feel like going jogging, or just want to sit on the grass on a nice day and sunbathe," Kyle said, coming to join me. He unlatched the French window and pushed it open so we could step out onto the balcony. "Though I tend to stay away from the park when West Ham are playing, because the crowds around the stadium before and after the game are unbelievable." He pointed off to his left. "If you look over there, you can see the canal. And if you walk along the towpath up to Hackney Wick, there are new bars and restaurants opening all the time. This area has really come up in the last few years, and I landed on my feet when I got this place. But I reckon about half of the flats in this development were snapped up by overseas investors before they were even finished."

He put an arm around my waist and pulled me back on to him. I felt the hardness of his cock pressing against me through the borrowed robe. He had to know I didn't have anything on underneath it, and if I'd had nowhere else to be, I'd more than willingly have let him take me back to bed so we could pick up where we left off the night before. Maybe even share a long, hot shower with him afterwards...

But the thought of Sheila expecting her delivery made me anxious. The coffee stall opened for business at ten, and even though she'd have croissants and cinnamon swirls to offer to any customers who arrived wanting breakfast, I didn't want to leave her waiting for her brownies any longer than I had to.

With reluctance, I slipped out of Kyle's embrace and went to dress, picking up my scattered clothes on the way to the bedroom. I finished the last of the coffee, brushed my teeth, and twisted my hair into a ponytail.

When I came back into the living room, Kyle had put on his jacket and was waiting for me, car keys in hand.

"Okay, let's get you home." He sounded like it was the last thing in the world he wanted to do, but I nodded and retrieved my handbag. I checked to make sure I wasn't leaving anything behind, then followed Kyle out of the flat and into the lift.

As we stepped out onto the pavement, Kyle pressed a button on his key fob and the hazard lights flashed on a nondescript silver Audi as the doors unlocked.

I settled myself in the passenger seat and fastened my seatbelt as Kyle eased the car away from the kerb.

He turned on the radio, flicking through stations until he came across one playing hits from the 1990s. We fell into a comfortable silence as he drove, and he made good time, taking a route through the side streets when we hit snarled-up traffic near Old Street Tube station.

"How do you know all these shortcuts?" I asked, as he swung a right turn, took us down a quiet back road past the campus of City University, and brought us out onto the main road once more. "Did you train to be a cab driver or something?"

He shook his head. "I've driven a lot in my job. Eventually, you get to learn the quickest route from A to B."

Again, he was maddeningly vague about what he did for a living, but I didn't press him on it. I supposed some people just didn't like talking about work.

Almost before I knew it, he brought the car to a halt in front of my apartment building.

"Here you are, my lady." He spoke in the gruff Cockney tones of the puppet chauffeur from *Thunderbirds*, and I giggled as he tipped an imaginary hat to me. "Are you going to need help loading your bike or anything?"

"No, I should be fine from here. But you've saved me so much time, honestly you have."

"For you, Millie, anything." His eyes shone with a dark intensity but a twinkle in his gaze lightened the moment. "So…"

I paused with my hand on the door handle of the Audi. "So?"

"Next time, cheese toasties?"

"From the stall on Borough Market? Yeah, that would be fun. Let me know when would be good for you."

I went to get out of the car, but something in his expression told me he wasn't ready to say goodbye just yet.

"Before you go inside, I'd really like your advice on one thing. I didn't mention this last night because we were having such a good time and there didn't seem like a right moment to bring it up, but I was talking to my mum and she told me more about her and Charlie

Fox, like she wanted to get things off her chest before..." He looked away for a moment and I waited for him to compose himself. "She doesn't think it would be a good idea if I had any contact with Charlie's family, but...it's something I've got to do, you know? At the funeral, I felt this strong pull towards them, like blood calling to blood, and I can't ignore it."

"Then you have to do whatever you think is right. It sounds like your mother is trying to protect you, Kyle, which I completely understand, but I think you know what decision to make. All I'll say is that you need to sort this out sooner or later, otherwise it'll keep eating away at you."

He nodded, his mouth set in a resolute line. "Thanks, Millie." He caught hold of my hand and pulled me into a hug. His kiss was slow and sweet, and I could have drowned in it.

With a distinct lack of enthusiasm, I broke the kiss and got out of the car.

"I'll call you," he said.

I stood for a moment, watching until the car had disappeared around the corner, then I turned and made my way up to my apartment.

Chapter Eight

Kyle

Millie was right. If I wanted to find out where I stood with the Fox family, I needed to do something sooner rather than later. I couldn't keep stewing in thoughts of what could have been, if only I'd discovered the truth about my dad before now.

I didn't expect to find any of the family listed on the electoral register, at least not the one that was available for the general public to view, so I started searching for information among my gangland contacts. The second of them I spoke to was happy to tell me where Lynda Fox lived in return for a handful of ecstasy pills. I had to smile when he gave me the address—I'd supplied drugs to a house further along the same street on more than one occasion.

I parked my car in the closest available bay to the Fox family home. Parking around here was strictly for residents and their visitors only, but my customers down the road had given me a handful of the paper permits the council dished out. It meant I'd be fine in the rare event a traffic warden wandered by when I was making a delivery. I stuck one to the windscreen and went to call on Lynda.

The street was quiet, respectable. I was sure the neighbours knew they had criminals living among them — with all the publicity Charlie Fox's murder had got, they couldn't fail to — but clearly none of them seemed to care. A woman emerged from one of the houses, wearing multi-coloured athleisure gear and with a rolled-up yoga mat under her arm. She unlocked her car and got in without even glancing in my direction. A council worker cut the grass in the garden at the heart of the square, the mower's engine a steady drone. It was all so much nicer than the council estate where I'd grown up, and I was gripped with envy, imagining the life Charlie's other children had.

I double-checked I'd got the right house, rang the doorbell and waited. When no one had answered after half a minute, I rang it again, a longer press than before, and followed that up by rapping the lion's head knocker. A muffled voice came from the other side of the door, sounding distinctly annoyed.

"All right, all right. I'm coming."

The door swung open and Lynda Fox, her face clean of make-up and her hair tied up in a leopard-print scrunchie, peered up at me. A brown cockapoo puppy stuck its snout out of the doorway and sniffed the air, and she shooed it back.

"Go on, Baby, get inside." The stare she fixed me with was downright hostile, and I found myself wondering how many unwanted visits she'd had from journalists in the days since Charlie had died. "Whatever you're selling, I'm not interested."

"I'm not selling anything," I assured her. I gave her my most winning smile, the one that never failed to melt the heart of any female from nine to ninety. Her stony expression didn't crack.

"If you're collecting for charity, we don't give at the door in this house, and if you're here on behalf of some church, well, I've got no time for organised religion, love. That ship sailed a *long* time ago."

"I'm not here for any of those reasons." I kept my tone level and reasonable, not wanting to antagonise her further. "I'm Kyle Ferguson. I'm here because my mother is Joanna Ferguson. She worked as a waitress at Cucina dell'Atore back in the nineties, and she knew your husband well. *Very* well, in fact."

Any colour drained from Lynda's already pale face, and she clutched the collar of her fuchsia velour tracksuit top. "Oh gawd, you… You're Charlie's kid. I should have known it the moment I saw you." She shook her head. "You've got his eyes."

My mouth had gone dry. I'd rehearsed the way this conversation would go as I drove over here, and now of all that had flown out of the window. Lynda looked as if she might collapse, and I put out a hand and caught hold of her elbow to steady her. For the first time, turning up on her doorstep out of the blue seemed like a mistake. I thought I'd been so clever, confronting her in the one place she couldn't run away from me and my questions, but now I saw her as a grieving widow who simply wanted to be left alone.

"I'm sorry," I began. "I shouldn't have come here…"

"No." Her voice had regained some of its initial firmness and she pulled herself up to her full height. "I should have known this would happen one day. The way Charlie went catting around, it's a wonder there aren't more of you running around out there with his blue eyes and his cocky manner. Why don't you come in? You could probably do with a cup of tea. I know I could."

"Thanks, that's very kind of you." *Way kinder than I deserve.*

She led me into a living room with big French windows that looked out onto a wooden deck and a walled garden beyond that. I sat on one of the overstuffed cream sofas, sinking into the soft cushions, and she left me alone while she went to make tea for both of us.

On the coffee table in front of me were a few photographs in silver frames. Judging by the empty spaces on the mantelpiece I guessed they usually occupied, I reckoned she'd been looking at them before I arrived. One was of Lynda and Charlie on their wedding day. I picked it up and studied it with interest. In the pictures the BBC had used when they'd been running news items on his death and funeral, Charlie had been in his sixties, grey-haired and overweight. Here, he was young and handsome in a shiny pale-grey suit, with a shock of blond hair and piercing blue eyes. Lynda's wedding dress had huge puffy sleeves and dozens of rows of small pearls sewn onto it, and they were gazing at each other with a look full of love and adoration.

I set the photo down and turned to the next one. Three boys of varying ages, all in matching school uniforms, looking as if it was a struggle for them to sit still long enough for the photographer to take the shot. Beside it was another picture of those same three boys, now grown up. I recognised them as the ones who'd carried Charlie's coffin into the church at the cemetery. The bond between the Fox brothers had been obvious to me that day and seeing this image of the three of them with their arms draped around one another's shoulders only reinforced how much they cared for one another. Envy gripped me, sharp and painful. Growing up, I'd longed to have a little brother or sister of my own, and I wanted what these three had so badly it hurt.

Lynda Fox came into the room carrying a tray, and I relaxed back in my seat, trying to make it seem like I'd been doing anything other than looking at those family portraits.

"Here you go. I brought the milk and sugar because I don't know how you take it."

"Thank you very much." I took the mug she offered me and added a splash of milk.

"Help yourself to biscuits." She gestured to a plate containing a selection of sweet treats. I picked out a caramel wafer in a shiny red and gold wrapper and nodded my thanks.

"So..." Lynda began, sitting opposite me and pouring milk into her own mug. "Your mother was the little tart at Cucina dell'Atore who Charlie was knocking off."

My hackles rose and I broke the wafer in half with a sharp snap. "My mum wasn't – isn't a tart."

She held a hand up in apology. "I'm sorry, I take it back. But what am I supposed to think when a stranger turns up on my doorstep and tells me he's the product of the affair I always thought Charlie was having but could never prove."

"Fair enough. I shouldn't have ambushed you like that. But I couldn't think of any other way to get to meet you, and after the funeral – "

Her eyebrows rose sharply. "You came to Charlie's funeral?"

"I had to. Even though I never knew him, I needed to say goodbye to him. You have to understand, I lived my whole life thinking my dad was someone who'd died before I was even born, then when I learned the truth, it raised this whole set of questions no one could answer for me. And I don't have very much time left with my mum..."

"Really?"

"She — she has cancer. They're looking after her at St Susan's in Hackney, but — "

"Oh, you poor boy." Lynda's tone had softened, no longer accusing me, and when she glanced my way, her eyes had a glassy sheen. "Well, I can understand why you'd want to know more about where you came from." She reached for a chocolate-covered biscuit and took a bite. Silence hovered between us, still holding a certain tension.

I was the first to speak. "I know you don't have any obligations towards me — I mean, I'm really surprised you didn't send me packing when I turned up here. And I don't want you thinking I'm here because I'm entitled to some of the inheritance or anything. But...when I was at Highgate, I saw you with all your family. I realised I didn't only have a dad I'd never met, I have half-brothers, too. And I was kind of hoping I could get to meet them as well."

I'd have understood it if Lynda had dismissed my request out of hand. I'd already upended her life by turning up on her doorstep unannounced and demanding to know more about my dead father. She'd have been perfectly within her rights to end things here. Instead, she looked at me for several moments, considering what I'd said, then gave a slow nod.

"I doubt my Charlie would have been so forgiving if you'd told him what you've just told me, and can you blame me for thinking you might reckon we owe you something. But…I look at you sitting there, and I see so much of you in him, the way he was when he was young. Is it wrong of me to want to hold on to that?"

I bit my lip. Lynda Fox seemed so much larger than life, but underneath her brash façade I could tell she must be as lost and confused as I was. I didn't know how to respond to her question. Luckily, I didn't have to.

"The boys will be coming round for Sunday lunch like they always do," Lynda told me. "I'd be delighted for you to join us. It'll be a good way for us all to get to know one another. And bring your wife along—if you're married, that is."

"I'm not. But I do have…" I hesitated. I could hardly call Millie my partner, given we'd only been on one date. But 'girlfriend' didn't sound right for the bond we already shared. "Someone special in my life."

"Well, bring them along then. We usually sit down for dinner at one on the dot."

With that, it seemed like the subject was at an end. I'd have to let Millie know we would be visiting the Foxes for lunch this Sunday.

Lynda helped herself to another biscuit and offered me the plate. I glanced at the clock on the mantelpiece and shook my head. "I'd love to, but I've got to get to a meeting." I didn't tell her it was with one of my suppliers, bringing me my cut of a consignment of cocaine that had come in through the docks at Tilbury last night. She didn't need to know I'd inherited more than just the colour of my eyes from Charlie Fox.

"Well, it was nice of you to drop by, and I look forward to seeing you on Sunday. I'm sure the boys will be pleased to meet you too."

I'm sure they will. I rose to my feet and let Lynda see me to the front door, leaving my tea half drunk and wondering whether I'd made the right decision in agreeing to meet all the family on her turf.

Chapter Nine

Kyle

I still had my qualms about meeting the Foxes en masse, even as I parked the car at the end of their street. It was as if I'd found myself playing a game where I didn't quite understand all the rules, and talking to Lynda Fox had left me with more questions than it had answered.

At least Millie had been happy to come to lunch with me. I had the feeling it was more about the opportunity it gave her to spend time with me than out of any desire to meet the members of North London's most notorious crime family.

As I fastened one of my visitor's permits to the windscreen, Millie got out of the car clutching a box of homemade red velvet cupcakes topped with fat swirls of cream cheese icing.

"And you're sure Lynda will like these?" she asked me for what must have been the hundredth time.

"Well, I don't know how anyone could fail to like your cakes, but yeah, she'll love them. I get the impression she's got a really sweet tooth, so those will be perfect." I kissed her cheek. "And you look beautiful."

"Thanks." Millie's pale skin coloured deliciously as she blushed. The weather was cool and overcast, and she'd dressed for the occasion in a navy-blue crocheted jumper and skinny jeans with her hair swept up and pinned on top of her head.

I kept my head down and looked straight ahead of me as we walked to Lynda's house. It was unlikely I would bump into my regular customers from the neighbouring house, but I didn't want to get into any awkward small talk if I did.

"Okay, here goes." I pressed the doorbell and waited. Lynda must have been keeping an eye out for our arrival, because she answered the door within seconds.

Unlike my previous visit to her home, she was all smiles. She'd also applied make-up, styled her hair and wore a black cashmere jumper with batwing sleeves and leopard-print leggings. "Kyle, lovely to see you. Do come in. And this is—?" She cast a quizzical look at Millie.

"I'm Millie, Mrs Fox. Kyle's girlfriend."

Lynda arched an eyebrow. I realised when I'd fudged the nature of my relationship with Millie and simply called her 'someone special', she must have jumped to the conclusion that I was gay, but didn't want to admit to it straight out. Still, all she said was, "Millie, darlin', what a pleasure to meet you, and please, call me Lynda," as she ushered us inside the house.

"We brought you something to say thank you for inviting us to lunch." Millie held out the box of cupcakes.

Lynda took it and removed the lid. She eyed the contents with an approving smile. "These look very nice. You got them from that lovely little bakery in Camden Passage, didn't you?"

Millie shook her head. "I made them myself this morning."

"That's what Millie does," I cut in. "She has a business selling cakes."

"Oh, so you've found yourself an enterprising one. Well, that's good." Lynda put an arm around my shoulder. "Come through to the dining room and I'll make the introductions. Everyone else is here already."

We followed her down the hallway and into a room dominated by a large round table. Half a dozen faces stared at us as we walked in, and I found myself reaching for Millie's hand and giving it a reassuring squeeze. Two of Charlie Fox's sons sat at the table, along with two women I didn't recognise and a couple of little girls. Their expressions ranged from curious to downright indifferent, like the row of judges in a TV talent show in the moment before they begin to tear the contestant's performance apart.

"Everyone, I'd like you to meet Kyle and Millie." She guided us to the two vacant seats on one side of the table. As we sat, she did a quick sweep of introductions. "This is my second eldest, Connor, and his wife Roz, and that's my youngest, Cameron, and his girlfriend Emily. And those are Connor's girls, Kelsey and Mia. My eldest, Callum, would have been with us, but his wife Naomi was in a car accident not too long ago and she's not feeling too well today."

I recalled the dark-haired woman with a pair of crutches I'd seen in the Fox family pew at the funeral. That must be Naomi. From the looks Connor and Cameron exchanged when their mother mentioned the accident, there was some story behind it. I wasn't sure I wanted to find out what that story was.

"Connor, would you pour our guests a drink? I'm just going to fetch the roast."

Lynda bustled out of the room, leaving Millie and me to face an inquisition from the two brothers.

"So, how come you know Mum, Kyle?" Cameron asked, leaning closer to me across the table. "She doesn't have a habit of inviting any old Tom, Dick or Harry round for lunch, so forgive us if we're a little surprised to see you here."

I took a breath. "There isn't an easy way to tell this story, but I'm here because…you, me, Connor and — Callum, is it? — we share a dad. Charlie Fox was my father."

"You what?" Connor said, as if he hadn't heard me properly. "Is this some kind of joke?"

"Yeah, which of the tabloids do you write for?" Cameron's tone was cold. "I mean, it's certainly an original angle, pretending to be some long-lost half-brother of ours we never knew about, but if this is all so you can write some sleazy story about Dad, you can get out of this house right now."

"It's not a lie," Millie spoke up, and I could have hugged her for her willingness to stand up for me against the combined hostility of the Fox brothers. "Kyle didn't know Charlie was his dad until very recently. I mean, if you can't see the resemblance…" She addressed Cameron head on. "I haven't met you or Connor before today, but when I look at you, then I look at Kyle, there's something so similar about all three of you, it's clear to me you're related."

"Charlie had an affair with my mother when she was nineteen," I went on. "She didn't tell me the truth because she was trying to protect me. I'm starting to think she shouldn't have bothered."

"Hey." Connor held up his hands in a placating gesture. "Look, we might have been too hasty—it wouldn't be the first time Cameron put two and two together and came up with five—but this is as much a shock for us as it must be for you. Here, let me get you that drink Mum mentioned." He waved towards the two bottles of wine in the centre of the table. "Red or white, Millie?"

"White, please." Millie relaxed in her seat, the defensive set of her shoulders easing.

Connor came round to Millie and filled her a glass with a generous amount of chardonnay. "What about you, Kyle?"

"I'll have red, thanks, but only a small one. I'm driving."

Roz gave me a sympathetic smile, and I realised she must be the designated driver in that couple. As Connor took the bottle of pinot noir and poured me a little, Lynda came back into the room carrying a platter bearing a large piece of roast pork topped with thick crackling. She seemed oblivious to any lingering tension in the room.

"Oh, Mum, that smells wonderful," Cameron said.

"Thanks, love." She beamed at the compliment as she set the food on the table. "Kyle, Millie, I hope you like pork." A thought appeared to occur to her. "Oh, you're not vegetarians, are you? I never thought to ask.

Though if you are, you can have some of that nut roast thing I made for Naomi, seeing as she's not here."

"Pork will be perfect," I assured her, "for both of us."

"In that case, Connor, would you like to do the honours?"

"Of course, Mum." Connor got up from his seat. He took hold of the carving knife and fork and set about slicing up the meat with panache, obviously relishing the role of being man about the house now his father was no longer around.

Millie looked at me over the rim of her wine glass and I gave her my most reassuring smile in return. Connor and Cameron Fox hadn't exactly welcomed us with open arms, but I could understand their reticence. I didn't know how I'd react if I was suddenly confronted with a family member I'd never known existed, particularly not one who was the product of an illicit affair.

As Connor moved from guest to guest, adding two thick pieces of crackling-topped pork to everyone's plate in turn, Lynda said, "Help yourselves to vegetables, everyone." She gestured to a couple of white porcelain tureens, and I removed the lid of the nearest one. It contained crisp, golden roast potatoes, and I served Millie before taking a few myself.

I passed the dish over to Emily, who took it with a murmured, "Thank you." The look she gave me made me think she, at least, was comfortable with my presence here, and I couldn't help wondering how recently she'd become a member of the Fox clan.

Once everyone had full plates, Lynda tapped the side of her wine glass with her fork, stilling the chatter around the table and drawing everyone's gaze to her.

"These have been a strange few weeks for all of us, but seeing you here today, welcoming Kyle and Millie, well, I think that deserves a toast." She raised her glass. "To family."

"To family," we all echoed.

"And to Charlie, who I will never stop missing," Lynda added, before she took a long swig of her chardonnay.

I sipped from my own glass, feeling uncomfortable about toasting the memory of the father I'd never known. Whoever had selected the wine had chosen well. This certainly wasn't cheap supermarket plonk. But then everything about this house suggested the Foxes had plenty of money and enjoyed spending it on the nice things in life.

"Well, dig in, everybody," Lynda instructed us. "Don't let your food go cold."

For a couple of moments, there were no sounds other than those of cutlery clinking against china, and the odd satisfied murmur as people savoured the roast dinner Lynda had cooked. As I looked around the table, the prospect of becoming a real part of this family seemed tantalisingly within reach.

Then Connor asked the question I'd been dreading. "So, Kyle, what is it you do for a living?"

"Oh, I'm in import-export." The line slipped out without my thinking. I noticed Cameron and Connor exchange a look and realised they knew my lie for what it was. They probably used the same term to describe their own activities.

"Really? Well, you might know some of the same people we do," Cameron said. "Like Phil O'Rourke? Joe Martindale? The Yianni brothers?"

I met each name with a blank stare, guessing either they were low-level criminals, or they ran the businesses the Foxes used to launder the proceeds of their crime. None of them meant anything to me, and if Connor and Cameron were setting up a trap for me, I was determined not to fall into it. "Sorry, never heard of them."

"Who was that bloke Charlie used to drink with in the Duke of Canklow who was in import-export?" Lynda appeared to be racking her brain. Eventually she clicked her fingers. "Eddie Oxley, that was it."

"Didn't you hear, Mum? Eddie got himself arrested last week," Connor said.

"Yeah, they got him on a charge of intent to supply," Cameron chipped in. "Apparently, he was hanging around trying to sell weed near the gates of Camden Hall. Isn't that right, Em?"

Emily nodded. "Every pupil at the school gets the talk about saying no to drugs as part of their PSHE lessons — that's personal, social, health and economic education, for any non-parents in the room," she added with a glance at me and Millie. "But they don't always take any of the information in."

"Well, anyone who peddles that filth to kids deserves whatever they get." Lynda's words dripped with real venom. When I met her gaze, unable to help wondering why this subject riled her so much, she added, "One of Charlie's best friends from school — his daughter fell in with a bad crowd and got addicted to heroin. She ended up dead from an overdose. She wasn't even eighteen years old..."

"With all respect," I replied. "Cannabis and heroin are two very different drugs. You're very unlikely to die just from smoking a few joints."

"Yeah, but you start off with a bit of cannabis and who knows what you'll end up taking. It's a — what do they call it? Gateway drug. Everybody knows that."

I wasn't going to argue with Lynda, not at her own dinner table. It seemed clear that as far as she was concerned, drug dealers were the lowest of the low — and, judging from Connor's and Cameron's expressions, they felt the same way.

"And what about you, Millie?" Roz's voice broke the growing tension in the room.

Millie immediately twigged what she was being asked. "I make brownies and sell them online, mostly. That's how I first got to know Kyle. He tried one of my cakes and liked it so much he just had to thank me for it."

"Well, Millie brought me some cupcakes," Lynda chimed in, "and I was thinking we could have them for dessert, seeing as Naomi was intending to cover the sweet course today." She took a moment to look around the table, as if she was counting up the number of guests in her head. "I think there'll be enough to go round."

The promise of cake seemed to encourage everyone to finish what was left on their plates, and when Lynda rose to start clearing the table, I offered to help her.

"Thanks, darlin', that's sweet of you."

I collected the empty dinner plates and trailed behind Lynda with them all the way to the kitchen, then helped her stack the dishwasher.

As I was returning to the dining room, Cameron emerged. He looked around to make sure his mother wasn't within earshot, then pushed me up against the wall. Anyone passing by might have thought we were just making friendly conversation, but his tone was anything but nice as he growled, "You might have got Mum eating out of your hand, but there's something I don't like about you, and I can't put my finger on it."

"Yeah?" His eyes were so like mine as he glared at me, it was as if I were looking in a mirror. I met the challenge in his gaze and kept my voice level. "Well, your mother's a nice woman, and I'd like to get to know her better. Emily, Roz and the girls, too. I've never had nieces I could spoil." He said nothing, and I went on, "I'm not doing this to get at you or your brothers. I simply want to understand where I've come from."

"Well, when you figure that out, maybe you can go back there." Cameron released his grip on my arm and went back into the dining room.

I slipped into my seat to find everyone 'ooh'-ing and 'aah'-ing over Millie's cupcakes. After the outright hostility I'd been shown by Cameron, it warmed my heart to see Millie getting a more welcoming treatment. A sneaky little voice in my head whispered that I should be using her as my 'in' to the Fox family, but I did my best to ignore it. I'd really fallen for her, harder and faster than I'd ever expected to, and I didn't want to do anything that would jeopardise our relationship.

Millie held out the remaining cakes and offered them to Cameron, then me. "There's one left for each of you."

"Have you finished yours?" I asked as I took one. When I glanced at her empty plate. I didn't see any sign of crumbs or the crumpled paper case the cupcake had been baked in.

"That's okay, Kyle. I didn't—" she began.

Typical Millie. She's prepared to go without to make sure I get mine. I honestly don't deserve her.

I was touched by the gesture, but I didn't want her to be the only one not enjoying dessert. "In which case…" I took a knife, sliced the cake down the middle and handed half to her.

Someone—it might have been Emily—murmured, "Oh, that's sweet."

I couldn't resist a look across at Cameron, trying to gauge his reaction to my gesture. I had no idea why it was so important to convince him I wasn't whatever kind of leech he'd pegged me as, but I'd gained the impression that out of all the Fox boys, he was his mother's favourite and the one whose opinion she would listen to.

Lynda pressed her napkin to her lips and wiped away a dab of icing. "Millie, darlin', I'm not just saying this, but that really was the best cupcake I've ever eaten."

A soft blush coloured Millie's cheek as she accepted the compliment. "Thank you so much, Mrs—Lynda."

"Can I get anyone tea or coffee?" Lynda asked.

Everyone started answering. Millie seemed about to make her own request for a drink, but I cut in, "We'd love to stay, really, and thank you so much for a delicious lunch, but I promised Mum we'd go and see her in the hospice this afternoon."

"Oh, of course, darlin'." Lynda's expression was fond. "Well, it's been lovely to meet both of you, and please do come over and see me again any time."

Millie flashed everyone a smile as she rose from her seat, but I could tell my sudden need to leave had confused her. We'd made no plans to visit Mum, and she had to know I was lying. Still, all she said was, "If you have any requests for cakes you'd like me to bring next time, let me know." She brought a business card out of her handbag and passed it to Lynda. "All my details are on there, including the website address. Take a look. It'll give you a better idea of what I make."

"Well, darlin', you can fetch round whatever you like if it's as good as that red velvet cake."

Lynda showed us to the front door, and we said our goodbyes on the doorstep. I was sure it wasn't my imagination that as she went back inside the house, Cameron stood in the hall, watching to make sure we were gone.

Chapter Ten

Millie

I turned to Kyle as he brought the car to a halt in front of my apartment building. "Would you like to come inside, or do you have somewhere else to be?"

"Nope, no other plans. And I'd love a drink if you were thinking of making one, seeing as we turned down Lynda's offer of coffee." The smile he gave me didn't quite reach his eyes, and I knew he needed to talk about whatever was bothering him. I had to be careful how I coaxed it out of him, though. He'd shown over lunch how prickly he could get when he was forced onto the defensive.

"Good, so maybe we can go in and discuss it."

"Discuss what?" He stabbed at the touchscreen on the dashboard to turn off the radio.

"Whatever's eating you up. Something happened at Lynda Fox's, and I don't know what it is but you're clearly stewing on it."

Kyle scrubbed a hand across his face. "I just wish things had gone better than they did."

"Funny, I thought they went pretty well."

"For you, maybe." He realised he'd reacted too sharply and softened his tone. "Cameron Fox doesn't like me. He made that very clear when we were both out of the room. I don't know what I've done to offend him, but—"

"You don't need to have done anything. He might be the youngest of the brothers, but he's clearly the ringleader of the three. Probably because he's the youngest—they're always the ones who can twist their mother round their little finger. And you turning up out of the blue like you did, well, he's bound to see that as a threat." Millie reached to unbuckle her seatbelt. "And we can keep talking about this in the car, but I'd far rather discuss it upstairs over a cup of coffee."

"Okay."

We got out of the car and went inside, greeting the weekend concierge as we passed. Kyle's shoulders were hunched and he thrust his hands deep in his pockets. I felt that if I touched him, he'd give off little sparks of hurt and annoyance.

In the lift, he leaned against the wall, taking slow, deep breaths. If it had been anyone else, I might have thought he was using some mindfulness technique to centre himself and calm his raging thoughts, but I knew Kyle didn't have any time for what he considered 'hippie nonsense.'

He didn't say a word as we got out on my floor. I let him into the apartment, and he marched straight to the living room and flung himself down on the couch.

"So, coffee with a splash of milk, no sugar, right?" I asked, following him in at a more sedate pace.

He grunted a 'yes' in reply.

"Find some music for us, would you?" I added. "I have the Spotify app on the TV. The remote should be on the coffee table." With that, I turned on my heel and went into the kitchen.

While I waited for the kettle to boil, I wondered what could have happened to affect Kyle so deeply it had caused to him to withdraw into himself.

It can't only be that Cameron Fox doesn't like him, surely? I know Kyle's used to charming everyone he meets, and Lynda seemed taken with him, but…

With a shake of my head, I reached for the packet of expensive Blue Mountain coffee that had been one of Amanda's 'just because' presents to me. I kept telling her she didn't need to give me any extravagant treats, that even though I'd turned my back on the finance world and the high salary it brought with it, I could still afford to buy nice things from time to time, but she had a generous streak a mile wide.

I made coffee and took the cafetiere, milk jug and mugs through to Kyle. He had selected a playlist titled 'quiet instrumental Sunday afternoon', and ethereal piano music drifted through the living room.

"Okay," I said, sitting on the couch by his side and pressing the plunger on the cafetiere, "are you ready to tell me what's eating you alive right now?"

Kyle put his head in his hands as I poured the coffee. Other people might have taken that as a no, but I wasn't going to let him sour the atmosphere with his sulky mood. When he looked up at me, I regarded him with a steady gaze. I hoped it conveyed my determination to get to the bottom of things.

"Nothing," he said at length as he picked up his coffee mug. "Only that Cameron accused me of not being who I said I was, and said I'd gone to his mother's home because I was trying to scam his family."

I let out a little snort.

Kyle glared at me. "What's so funny?"

"I find it hard to believe that a man who, by every account, is involved in all manner of criminal activity would accuse someone else of being a scammer."

"Think what you like, but the Foxes are really protective of their turf. Did you not hear about what happened to the last guy who tried to muscle in on their territory?"

"No, what?"

"Oh, it was some small-time thug from Liverpool." Kyle bit his lip, clearly racking his brain for the man's name. "McMahon, yeah, that was it. Danny McMahon. Anyway, he started undercutting one of their rackets, got into a confrontation with Cameron Fox and ended up dead."

My eyes went wide. "Cameron killed him?" I could imagine the Fox brothers being capable of many things, but murder? It seemed a step too far, even for them.

"No, he was hit by a lorry. I don't know any more of the details than that, and I don't want to. All I'm saying is, you don't want to get on the wrong side of the Fox brothers. Bad things happen if you do."

"And I don't think you are." I took a sip of my coffee, mulling over what Kyle had told me. "If Cameron is wary of you, I suppose that's only to be expected. Even if he knew his dad had an affair all those years ago, it's one thing to be aware it happened, and another to learn there was a child as a result of it. And to meet that child out of the blue like he did today – "

"Yeah, I get it." Kyle's posture had grown less stiff, his shoulders settling back into their natural position rather than hunched up around his ears. "But I still had to visit them, you know? When Mum goes…" He swallowed, his Adam's apple bobbing. He appeared to be fighting back whatever unwanted thoughts threatened to surface. "When she's not here any longer, the Foxes will be the only blood relations I have, and if they disown me…"

"You'll still have me," I assured him, laying a hand on his arm. I set down my mug. "Whatever happens with your mother, I promise you won't have to face it alone."

"Thanks, Millie." For the first time since we'd arrived back at the apartment, his expression softened. He reached out and ran his fingertip along my bottom lip, tracing its contours. "That means a lot to me."

His face was so close to mine. His blue eyes were filled with longing. There was no resisting my attraction to him. I dropped a gentle, teasing kiss to the corner of his mouth, then another, encouraging him to open up to me. He swept me into his arms, and we rolled together on the couch.

"Damn, you do something to me," he muttered in my ear. His kisses were hot, urgent, and I went liquid at his touch. After all the stress of lunch with the Foxes, I knew I needed to make him feel good.

I pulled out of his arms and got to my knees on the floor. Before Kyle had time to work out what I intended, I had pushed him into a sitting position on the couch and was undoing his belt buckle.

"Hey, what are you—?"

I tugged down his zip, the metal teeth separating with a satisfying rasp, then reached into his underwear and brought out his already hardening cock.

"Just relax, Kyle. The next few minutes are going to be all about you."

When I bent my head and took the tip of his dick between my lips, he made a strange little noise, somewhere between a surprised chuckle and a sob. I glanced up at him with heavy-lidded eyes and ran my tongue over his cockhead. Salty pearls of pre-cum gathered there and I licked them away.

"Oh yeah, keep doing that."

Spurred on by Kyle's encouraging words and groans, I swallowed more of him down. The clock ticked on the mantelpiece, the music on the playlist had changed to a soaring violin sonata and I let myself float in the moment. I relished the taste of Kyle, the feel of him in my throat, and I knew I was in total charge of his pleasure.

When I brought my head up, threatening to let him slip from between my lips entirely, he looked down at me with a pleading gaze. I smiled at the sight of my brick-red lipstick, smeared in a ring around his shaft. Even though I knew it wouldn't last, I'd left my mark on him.

"Please, Millie, don't stop." Kyle sounded desperate, and I put an end to his agony by taking him even deeper into my mouth. I dug my fingers into his thighs through the thick denim of his jeans and sucked on him with an intensity I'd never known I possessed.

He wriggled on the couch, and when I looked up, he was trying to ease his jeans off his hips without letting his cock fall out of my mouth. I bit back a giggle at the mix of concerted effort and frustration on his face and gave him a hand. Once they were down below his knees, along with his underwear, I went back to licking and stroking him. The rich, musky scent of him hit me harder than before, fuelling my desire to make him come.

As his excitement grew, he thrust hard into my throat, and I gripped him tight around the base of his shaft, making sure he couldn't go any faster or deeper than I was comfortable with. This might be all about satisfying his needs, but he still needed to be aware that I was the one setting the pace.

"Oh, so good," he groaned, then he gave up trying to form words as I cupped his tight balls with my other hand. He pulled the pins out of my updo, releasing it to fall around my face. As I bobbed my head, the ends of my hair wafted over the insides of his thighs, tickling the sensitive skin there. My cheeks hollowed as I sucked harder and my tongue danced over his swollen cockhead. His hips jerked, losing any kind of rhythm, and I knew he had to be close to coming.

I was using every little trick I knew in my attempts to wring out every drop of his pleasure, and when I traced a fingertip over the spot between the root of his dick and his balls, then down and around his puckered hole, he couldn't hold back. With a despairing groan, he shot his cum into my mouth, gripping my head to hold it in place as he came. Hot, thick jets hit the back of my throat as I did my best to swallow them down.

Spent, he collapsed back against the couch cushions. I rose, wiping the last salty traces of his orgasm from my lips with the back of my hand.

He shook his head, as if he wanted to say something but didn't have the energy left to speak. I curled up beside him, and he ran his fingers gently through my mussed-up hair.

"Everything okay?" I asked.

"Mm," he answered at length. "I honestly don't know what I've done to deserve you, Millie, but I'm so glad you're here right now. And I don't know where you learned to use your mouth like that, but wow…"

I didn't know whether I'd managed to chase away the demons that so clearly haunted him following our lunch with the Foxes. Meeting Lynda and her sons seemed to have raised far more questions than it had answered. But I knew that was a conversation we could have some other time. I had been able to soothe Kyle and make him feel good, even if only for a little while, and nothing else mattered.

I rested my head on his shoulder and listened to the sound of his breathing as it slowed and evened out. Within moments, he was asleep, his expression as untroubled as I hoped his dreams were.

Chapter Eleven

Millie

"So, what time does your train leave tomorrow?" Kyle asked, slipping back into bed beside me. He'd been out to the kitchen to make tea for both of us, and as I wrapped my hands around the mug and watched little wisps of steam rise into the air, I thought I'd be happy to wake up to this kind of treatment every morning.

"I'm booked on the 10.14 from Euston—I'll get into Manchester Piccadilly at lunchtime and then get the tram over to my parents' house. I'm just about packed already. I only need to finish wrapping the presents and I'm done."

"You still buy Christmas presents for your mum and dad? That's sweet."

I glanced at him, trying to work out whether he was teasing me, but his expression seemed sincere.

"Do you mind if I put the radio on?" I asked, reaching over to pick up my phone. "I want to catch the travel news, make sure I won't get caught up in any tailbacks when I take those cakes up to Highgate Grounds."

"Can you not just look at a website for that?" Kyle asked. It seemed a strange thing to ask, given that he was usually more than happy to wake up to music and the chatter of the Smooth Radio DJ, then I twigged the source of his reluctance.

"You're playing that stupid Wham! game, aren't you?"

"Yes, and I only have to go another couple of days without hearing *Last Christmas* anywhere, then the barman in the Fox and Crown will owe me twenty quid." He shrugged. "What can I say? A bet's a bet."

"It's a pity I won't be around to see you collect your winnings. Though I have to admit, after all this time we've been spending together, it's going to feel strange celebrating Christmas apart. But you could still come up to Manchester with me. My parents are so keen to meet you." I sat a little straighter in bed. My mother would relish nothing more than the opportunity to fuss over Kyle, but I wasn't going to tell him that right now. "A last-minute train ticket won't be cheap, mind. But I suppose you could always drive up and meet me there."

Kyle sighed. "I wish I could, but I promised Mum I'd spend Christmas Day with her. After all, this is probably the last one she'll be here for…"

I clapped a hand to my mouth as the realisation of what I'd said sank in. "Oh, Kyle, I'm sorry. That was so insensitive of me, wanting to drag you up north when —"

He cut me off with an airy wave. "It's okay. I know you didn't mean anything by it. And I'm sure I'll get to see your folks in the new year."

"Speaking of the new year, I was thinking it's finally time I took the plunge and started looking for somewhere to open those business premises I've been talking about. I've been browsing the listings from a couple of local letting agents, and there often seem to be little cafés available. Though it's all going to depend on how much rent they're charging—the ones I'd be able to afford are a lot farther out of the centre of Islington than I'd like."

"Yeah, but there are already lots of places around Upper Street selling fancy cupcakes and stuff. If you go somewhere where there's less competition, it'll be easier to establish yourself."

I nodded, conceding his point. My ultimate dream was to have a café close to all the nice antique shops and vintage clothes stores on Camden Passage, but from everything I'd seen online the area was well out of my price range, and I had to acknowledge that. "You're right, of course, but it would have been nice to go where people are already in the mood to spend money."

"Trust me, Millie, once they find out how good your brownies are, they'll start beating a path to your door even if you're right at the far end of the Northern Line. And I don't know how you're sorted for finances, but if you need any help, I'd be more than happy to come in with you as a partner."

"Seriously?" I wanted to make sure Kyle wasn't kidding around. My business was trading in the black, and I'd made sure to put aside what I would owe in tax this year. What would eat into my reserves would be all the extra equipment I would need when I scaled up my baking to meet the demands of supplying customers every day, and any cosmetic improvements my new premises would need. Kyle's help could really make a difference.

"What can I say?" Kyle shrugged. "Business is good right now. I have a lot of regular customers, and Christmas is one of my busiest times of the year. If you need a few grand to help you get this dream of yours off the ground, that shouldn't be a problem."

It was an offer of help beyond my wildest dreams. "Thanks, and I promise I'll pay you back as soon as I can…"

"Whoa, don't start worrying about that. You concentrate on finding the right place and when you have, we'll make an appointment to view it together. Trust me, Millie, this could be the start of something really special for you — for us."

A warm glow filled me as he talked about there being an 'us'. Even in the few weeks we'd been together, I'd grown closer to him than I could ever have imagined. The spark I'd felt when we'd met at the cemetery had ignited into something fierce and all-consuming. But I was still afraid to admit, even to myself, quite how deeply I'd fallen for him until I had some indication that he felt the same way. I didn't want to give my heart to him when he could so easily break it.

Still, Kyle's words had given me the confidence I needed to take the next step when it came to my business. "Okay, so when I'm back from Manchester, I'll get in touch with the letting agents, find out what they have that's in my price range, and I'll sort out a time to view any places I think might be suitable."

"Great, and I'll be right behind you on this, Millie. Nothing will make me happier than seeing you succeed — apart from you promising you won't listen to any Christmas songs while I'm around. Just in case."

I swatted him with my pillow as he chuckled to himself, then went out to the bathroom.

Chapter Twelve

Millie

Kyle strode down the hallway, a day's growth of dark stubble on his chin and a camouflage-patterned rucksack slung over one shoulder. I leaned in the doorway, my heart beating a little faster as I watched him approach. I wondered whether I'd ever lose the tingle of excitement that surged through me whenever we were together.

"Hi, babe." He scooped me up into a hug and pressed a long kiss to my lips. He smelled of fresh sweat and bergamot cologne, and I thought I could breathe the scent of him in forever. "Sorry I'm late. I tried to get here sooner, but...work, you know?"

In these early days of the new year, 'work' had become his standard explanation whenever I didn't hear from him, but I understood. If you were your own boss, things cropped up all the time that you had no way of delegating to anyone else. And it wasn't as if he didn't make up for his unexpected absences when we were finally together.

"It's okay, honestly." I ushered him inside the apartment. "Dinner's almost ready. I just need to heat up the bread rolls."

"Well, whatever you're making, it smells great." He slipped the rucksack off his shoulder, opened it up and presented me with a bottle of wine. "Hopefully this will go okay with it."

I studied the label. "Mm, cabernet sauvignon. I'll open it and let it breathe for a while. You go take a seat in the living room."

Kyle went to shrug off his jacket and stopped. He brushed his hands over his sides. "Shit, I think I've left my phone in the car. I'd better go down and check." He dropped the rucksack on the hallway floor. "I'll be back in a minute."

He set off back towards the lift at a trot, and I went to uncork the wine. I was on my way to the kitchen when I heard a phone ringing from somewhere behind me. It wasn't the familiar jangling tune of my phone, and anyway, that was on the kitchen table where I'd been using it to listen to music while I cooked. I turned and walked to where Kyle had dumped his bag, the sound growing louder as I did.

Don't tell me, he dropped his phone in there and forgot about it. I know he says he's working too hard, but...

I picked up the rucksack, thinking I could shout after him and save him a wasted trip down to his car. But when I unzipped it, any thoughts of calling Kyle faded to nothing. What I pulled out of the bag wasn't his familiar top-of-the-range iPhone. Instead, I held what he always referred to as a 'brick', the kind of phone that was incapable of being used for anything other than making calls, sending text messages or trying to beat your own high score on Snake.

"What the heck is he doing with this?" I muttered to myself, even though I wasn't sure I wanted the answer to that question. Of course, there could be an innocent explanation. It could be nothing more sinister than a backup in case the iPhone died on him. But somehow, I knew that wasn't the case. I should have simply dropped the phone back in his bag and tried to forget I'd seen it, but something compelled me to dig further inside.

Nausea rose in my throat as I pulled out more items and placed them on the floor. He was carrying around another three basic mobile phones and a dozen or more fat bundles of fifty-pound notes.

I don't know how long I sat in the hallway, staring at the contents of his rucksack. I had no idea exactly why Kyle had any of these things in his possession, but a series of reasons swam into my mind, none of them good.

"Millie..." Kyle's voice broke me out of my trance. I'd left the door ajar for him, but I hadn't heard him come back into the apartment. "What are you doing?"

"I could ask you exactly the same thing." My voice cracked as I held up the brick phone. "Why do you have this? And all the others, come to that. Nobody needs five different phones. And the money..."

His eyes were narrowed, his face clouded in an expression I'd never seen from him before. "Why are you poking around in what isn't yours?"

It wasn't the way I'd expected him to react. The cool, controlled anger in his tone had tears rushing to my eyes. He'd made it all too obvious I'd crossed a line, and I reacted with a panicked sob. "I heard a phone ring, and I thought you'd left your phone behind, that's all. I wasn't snooping deliberately, if that's what you think."

"But now you've seen it. Now you know what I am." He bent and snatched up the backpack from the floor.

My heart thudded in my chest. I'd never been so vulnerable as I was right now, even though I'd been naked and exposed to Kyle so many times. On those occasions, I'd known he would never do me any harm. Now, I wasn't so sure. Still, I refused to be cowed by him. "I don't know anything. But I can make a wild guess. Because the only people I've ever heard of who had this many different phones on them at once had either stolen them or needed them because they were dealing drugs." A cold, hard look crossed his face, and I knew one of the accusations I'd thrown out had to be correct. "Which is it, Kyle? Are you a thief or a dealer? At least have the decency to tell me the truth."

"I'm a dealer, okay?" he snarled. "Happy now?"

"No, not at all." My voice shook as I tried to come to terms with what he'd admitted to me. I should have realised, every time he'd answered one of my questions about what he did for a living with some vague answer, that he was hiding something from me. I thought of all the times he'd said he had somewhere to be, someone to meet, but been evasive when I'd pressed for more details. His preference for paying in cash, doing everything he could to minimise the evidence of where we'd been and what we'd bought. The signs had been there all along. I'd simply chosen to ignore them. "For Christ's sake, Kyle, why didn't you say anything before now?"

"Oh, and when would you have liked me to say something? It's not the kind of topic you bring up on a first date, is it? And I kept quiet because I thought this is how you'd react. I knew you wouldn't understand."

"What is there to understand? You sell drugs. It's not exactly rocket science."

"Yeah, and that's the problem." As he spoke, he began shoving everything back into the rucksack, as if he thought removing the wads of cash from my view would make the problem go away. "You'd love it if I was a rocket scientist, or some other fancy profession your parents could brag about."

"Excuse me?" I got to my feet. Now Kyle was the one crossing lines. "My parents have nothing to do with this."

"Of course they do. You were brought up in a nice middle-class home where you knew you'd never have to do anything you weren't proud of to earn money. You can't even begin to understand why someone might end up in a life of crime, or why people are looking for what I sell."

"I used to have a job in the City, remember? Twelve-hour days, week in, week out, under constant pressure. And most people in that environment played as hard as they worked, so yes, I'm completely aware of why there's a market for your...product. Oh, no one in the office would ever admit to snorting coke in the toilets, but everyone knew it went on. I just never wanted any part of that lifestyle." I let out a bitter laugh. "And the irony's staring you in the face, Kyle. You're so desperate to be part of the Fox family, yet despite all the awful things they've done and all the time they've spent in jail for them, they'd still want nothing to do with you if they found out you deal drugs."

"That's a low blow," Kyle muttered, but he couldn't deny that I spoke the truth. Though I didn't want to ruin whatever chance he had of connecting with his half-brothers, I just didn't know if I could stand to be around him now that I'd discovered how he earned his money.

"I think you'd better leave." Somehow, I found the strength to open the front door.

"This is it? You're breaking up with me?"

"I…" Was I? Could I really bear the thought of never seeing Kyle again? "I think it's best if we don't see each other for a while. This—" I waved an arm at the rucksack he clutched to his chest. "It's a lot to process."

"But this isn't the end?" The hurt in Kyle's eyes was too much to bear.

"Goodnight, Kyle."

I shut the door behind him and cried until no more tears would fall.

Chapter Thirteen

Millie

I arrived at the school where Emily taught as classes were letting out for lunch. Groups of teenagers spilled out through the front carpark, chatting and laughing at whatever they'd called up on their phones. A boy with his hands thrust deep in his pockets walked past me, the faint thump of hip-hop coming from his Bluetooth headphones. I found the last available space in the nearest cycle rack and chained up the cargo bike.

Ahead of me was the main school building, a tall Victorian redbrick construction with high windows and pointed gables, but the path was barred by a heavy iron gate. Above an intercom with a single buzzer was a sign reading *'WOULD ALL VISITORS PLEASE REPORT TO THE MAIN RECEPTION'*.

Apprehension seized me as I pressed the buzzer. All I knew about Emily was where she worked and though paying her an unexpected visit on her lunch break might not have been the wisest plan, it was the only one I had.

"Hello?" a woman's voice said through the crackle of the intercom.

"Hi, I have a delivery for one of your staff." I tried my best to sound like a typical delivery rider, bored and eager to be on the way to my next drop-off.

"Bring it through to reception, please. We're in the admin building, straight ahead of you."

With a click, the lock on the gate disengaged and I pushed it open. The voice had directed me to a squat, modern, glass-fronted building. It looked as out of place in these surroundings as I felt.

Inside, the heating was turned up a little too high for the warmth of the day, and from somewhere in the back of the reception area came the rhythmic whine of a photocopier churning out pages.

"Yes?" The middle-aged black receptionist on the other side of the pale wood desk glanced up from the Sudoku puzzle she'd been working on and regarded me over the rims of her glasses.

"Er, hi. I'm here with a lunch delivery for Emily Keating in the English department."

She nodded like this was a regular occurrence for the school's members of staff. "Up the stairs to the first floor and the staff room's down the hall on your left."

I didn't ask what I should do if Emily wasn't there, but the receptionist had already returned to filling in the last couple of blank spaces on her puzzle grid, so I mumbled a thank-you and followed her instruction.

Hovering by the staff room door, I wondered whether I should knock or simply walk in. My dilemma was solved when a youngish man with wild curly hair and a gingery beard emerged into the corridor, pulling the strap of a backpack onto his shoulder.

"Excuse me, do you know if Emily Keating is in there?" I held the small, insulated bag I'd packed with goodies for her — food I'd told myself absolutely wasn't a bribe in return for the advice I needed — and he regarded it with a knowing smile.

He turned and bellowed into the depths of the staff room, "Hey, Em. Have you been ordering off Deliveroo again? You know that's a quid you owe the end-of-term booze-up fund." With a shake of his head, he told me, "Everyone says at the start of term they'll bring lunches from home every day to save money, but then I suppose if they did, you guys would be out of work."

Grateful my ruse had worked, I offered him a swift, "Cheers, mate," and went inside.

Emily sat in a utilitarian, grey-upholstered armchair, drinking from a mug with a cartoon elephant on it. I studied her as I approached. The first time we'd met, I wondered how someone so outwardly respectable, with such a responsible job, could have become involved with a gangster like Cameron Fox. I hoped her answer to that question would help me clear my confusion about Kyle.

I cleared my throat as I came to stand by her chair. "Hi, Emily."

She looked up, confusion clouding her features. "Millie? What are you doing here? There must be some kind of mix-up. Whatever Andy thinks, I haven't ordered any food."

"I know, but it was the only way I could think of to get to see you away from the Foxes. And I really need to talk to you." I pulled open the Velcro fastening of the lunch bag and fished out two foil-wrapped packages.

"Here, I brought you a chocolate orange brownie and a couple of spinach and feta pasties, seeing as I'm thinking of branching out into savoury options. I'd really like your opinion on everything."

"Thanks, that's so nice of you, but you really didn't have to." She unwrapped a corner of the foil surrounding the brownie. "Though I have to say, this does look very nice." Clearly tempted despite herself, she broke a small piece off and popped it in her mouth. Her eyes went wide as she chewed. "Oh, my God. This is amazing. Seriously, Millie, give some of these to Lynda and she'll love you forever."

Her words reminded me I had never taken Lynda up on her offer to go round for coffee or treated her to the cakes I'd promised. "I'll see what I can do. I'm always looking for guinea pigs to try my new products."

"Well, she's still raving about those red velvet cupcakes you took over for Sunday lunch. And if you're seriously looking for feedback, this gets my seal of approval. It's got just the right amount of gooiness in the middle…" She helped herself to another bite, bigger than the first. "Can I get you something to drink?"

"I'd love a cup of tea, but" — I glanced around at the other teachers, some eating their lunches, others working their way through a stack of papers on their laps — "isn't someone going to realise I'm not supposed to be here?"

Emily shook her head. "As long as I put some money in Andy's party fund, no one's going to pay the slightest bit of attention to what we're doing, I promise. Now, take a seat and I'll get you that tea. How do you take it?"

"Milk, no sugar, please."

She wandered over to a table that held a filter coffee machine and a mismatched assortment of cutlery and switched on a jug kettle. As she waited for the kettle to boil, I toyed with the fringe of my scarf, still unable to shake the feeling that I'd intruded on some private inner sanctum. I should have found some other way to spend time with Emily, taken her to a coffee shop where we could sit and chat away from people she knew, but my thoughts were still so jangled after everything I'd discovered about Kyle's criminal career.

"Here you go." Emily held out a floral-patterned mug to me, bringing me back out of my musings.

"Thank you." I took a sip of my tea while she settled herself in her chair.

She fixed me with a soft look. "Now, what was it you wanted to talk to me about?"

I took a breath, not sure where to begin, but when I started to speak, the words tumbled out of me like they would never stop. "Kyle left this bag in my apartment, and I know I shouldn't have opened it, but…when I did, it was full of phones and money. That's when he admitted to me that he's a drug dealer. And I know I should have seen the signs, but I was starting to think he really was the one for me, so I guess I just ignored all the red flags." My voice cracked, and I swiped away the tears that threatened to fall. "And now, I don't know what to do. I told him to get out of my home, but…"

"But you're desperate to be with him. I know." Emily's tone was soothing, like she really understood what I was going through. "That's how it was with Cameron and me. I mean, as far as I know he's never been involved with drugs, but not long after we got together, I realised he was laundering money through various businesses and running all kinds of rackets with his brothers. I did my best to pretend I'd never seen anything, and I could put that part of his life to one side and none of it was my problem, right up until the point where Charlie Fox was shot dead in front of me."

"You were there when that happened?" I clamped a hand to my mouth, almost unable to comprehend how terrible it must have been. "Emily, I never knew. How do you get over something like that?"

Emily attempted a laugh, as if trying to brush aside the memory. "It's not easy. But I knew I needed to be strong for Cameron, and he was there for me, too."

"So, how do you do it? How do you live with the fact that your partner's a villain?"

She sighed, clutching her mug a little tighter. "Well, you have to reach a compromise with yourself and put up with the bad for the sake of the good. At least, that's what I do. I can't speak for Roz or Naomi, but they've been with Connor and Callum a lot longer than I've been dating Cameron. Hell, they have children with them, so they must have made their peace with it at some point. And let's face it, you've been to Lynda's house, you've seen the kind of lifestyle the family get out of it. Not everyone is able to walk away from that." She bowed her head for a moment, unable to meet my gaze. "I thought I would be able to, but in the end..."

"Yeah, I can appreciate that," I murmured, thinking of how much I'd missed everything I had with Kyle, and how hard it was proving to cut him out of my life for good.

"And don't get me wrong," Emily went on. "I have a great thing going with Cameron, and we love each other to bits. Whatever might happen, I know he'll be there for me. I don't think it's any exaggeration to say he'd die for me. If Kyle feels the same way about you, and you know he's the man you want to be with, then you have to decide whether you can separate the criminal part of him from the rest." She reached and took my hand. "No one will blame you if you decide it isn't worth the lies you'll have to tell yourself, or the things you'll have to overlook for the sake of being together, but bad people can have good hearts."

She seemed about to add something else, but a Scottish-accented voice yelled over from the other side of the staff room, "Hey, Em. Don't forget we've got that meeting with Jacqui about the lesson plans for the rest of the term."

Emily looked over in the direction of the comment. "I'll be with you in a minute, Clive." She rose to her feet and started gathering up the rest of the food I'd brought her into her bag. "Sorry, I've got to rush. The head of department here is nice enough, but she never likes to be kept waiting." She reached into her bag and pulled out a scrap of paper and a pen, then wrote down a series of numbers and handed the paper to me. "Phone me if you ever need to talk."

"Em," the man she'd referred to as Clive called again. "You ready? I don't want another bollocking because we're running late."

I got to my feet, our conversation officially at an end, and Emily gave me a hug. "Take care of yourself, Millie. And if you need anyone to try out those cakes of yours, I can always make myself available."

With that, she dashed over to join Clive, leaving me to make my way back down to where I'd left my bike. I didn't know that I was any closer to deciding about Kyle, but I felt better for having spoken to Emily. I slipped her phone number into my pocket and smiled, thinking I might have found myself the best ally I could in this crazy new world I'd been plunged into since meeting Kyle.

Chapter Fourteen

Kyle

Mum was dozing when I went into her room in the hospice. The monitors showing her vital signs hummed softly and the magazine she'd been reading was still open by her side. I went to put it on the bedside table, out of the way. It was open at the horoscope page, and though I'd never believed in the power of star signs to rule your life, I couldn't resist a glance at what the future apparently held in store for me.

A relationship may be on the line this week, Aries. Hurtful words are easy to say and hard to take back, but if you look in your heart, you'll know how to make things right. An impulsive getaway could be on the cards for you – if so, make sure not to leave your passport at home...

"What a load of rubbish," I muttered under my breath as I closed the magazine, trying not to think how

closely the forecast mirrored my situation with Millie.
Though it was wrong when it talked about travel plans.
I didn't intend to go any farther than Central London
over the next few days—Mum was so much weaker
than the last time I'd visited her, and all I could think
about was staying close by in case the worst happened.

She shifted in the bed and groaned like something
had disturbed her. I pulled a chair up close and took
hold of her ice-cold fingers, careful not to disturb the IV
tube inserted into the back of her hand and held in
place there with a thin strip of tape. Her papery skin
seemed even paler than before, the fine blue veins all
too visible through it.

"Hey, Mum, how are you doing?"

At first, I thought she hadn't heard me. Then her
eyes fluttered open and she gave me a weak smile.

"Hello, Kyle, love. I didn't hear you come in. I must
have fallen asleep."

"Are you okay? Do you need me to get you
anything?"

"Some water would be nice, thanks."

I poured a little from the jug by her bed into a plastic
beaker and helped her to drink it. I hated seeing her like
this, hated how the cancer continued to diminish her,
but I knew she would keep resisting its progress for as
long as she could.

Her thirst sated, I plumped up her pillow and
helped her into a more comfortable sitting position.
"That better?" I asked, as I plopped myself back down
on a chair.

"Much, thanks." She was putting on a brave face for
me—I couldn't help but notice how she winced every
time she moved, and pain clouded her gaze. I thought
about calling for a nurse to check in on her, but I knew

if she'd already had her dose of morphine, there was nothing else that could be done for her until she was due for the next one. "So, how are you, love? When are you fetching your girlfriend to see me?"

Until she brought it up, I'd forgotten I'd promised Millie would come with me the next time I visited her. "About that... Millie and I had a bit of a falling-out."

Her face sank, the lines around her eyes deepening. "Oh, Kyle, I'm sorry to hear it. Nothing serious, I hope."

"I—I did something she didn't like."

"Oh?" She fixed me with the sharpest glare she could manage, clearly not convinced by my bland explanation.

I heaved a sigh, knowing I could never keep anything from Mum. She'd always been able to wriggle all my little secrets out of me with nothing more than a look, ever since I'd been a kid. "I wasn't entirely truthful with her about how I earn a living. She wasn't happy about it."

"I can't say I blame her," Mum said with a sniff. "You know I've never approved, either, but I suppose when you've got Charlie Fox's blood running through your veins... At least you always had the grace to keep your dealing away from me when you were living under my roof, and what you do in your place is your affair. Though I'd hoped you'd have better sense than to mess on your own doorstep."

I couldn't meet her gaze. Even now I was in my late twenties, I still hated feeling that I'd let my mother down. Though she was right. I had never done anything that might bring unsavoury elements to her door, and I'd been determined I would show Millie the same respect. But, given how we'd parted, it was probably too late for that.

"I thought I could keep that side of my life from her." The words sounded hollow as I said them, and I realised again how foolish I'd been. Millie was sharp, observant. Even if she hadn't found out in the way she did, sooner or later she would have cottoned on to the fact that I earned a less-than-honest living. "And I regret that so much. But if I'd told her the truth right from the start, I don't think we'd have made it to the end of our first date."

"Are you sure? There are lots of girls out there who think they can change a man, turn him around and set him on the straight and narrow." Mum sounded as if she spoke from experience. I guessed she was talking about Charlie, and I knew how that had turned out.

"Millie's not the type. She's got her head screwed on and she won't stand for any bullshit. That's why I liked her so much."

"And you still do, don't you?" Mum reached for my hand and gave my fingers a gentle squeeze. I did my best not to notice how much even that little action took out of her. "Well, if you think she's worth fighting for, I say give it a go. I'm not guaranteeing you'll get anywhere with her, but if you have the chance, tell her how you feel. Let her know how much she means to you. If she still wants nothing to do with you, then at least you'll be sure where you stand."

"Thanks, Mum. Maybe you will get to see her before too long."

"I hope so, love. It's about time you found the right woman. And I always hoped I'd be around long enough to see you walk down the aisle…"

I wanted to tell her she still might be, but we'd both know that was a lie. Instead, I blinked away the tears that threatened to form and reached for the magazine Mum had been reading.

"I see you were looking at your horoscope," I commented. "Anything exciting in the stars for you?"

"To be honest, love, I don't remember. I think I fell asleep. Why don't you read it out for me?"

"Okay." I flipped to the right page and cleared my throat. "Virgo. *Something hidden away in your attic, basement or the back of a drawer could be worth more than you think. Now's the time to look for those old keepsakes you've forgotten about so they can realise their true potential. Who knew decluttering could be such fun?*" I set the magazine aside. "Well, that's a load of rubbish. I mean, you don't even have a basement..."

Mum chuckled, the sound rapidly turning to a dry, rattling cough. I grabbed the water glass and put it to her lips so she could sip from it. "Oh, Kyle, I don't know what I'd do without you around to keep me laughing."

And I don't know what I'll do without you...

She settled back against the pillow and closed her eyes. I sat with her until she fell asleep once more, mulling over in my mind what I should do about Millie. Mum was right. If I didn't at least attempt to set things straight between us, that would mean I didn't think she was worth fighting for. And nothing could be further from the truth. I just had to be prepared for the possibility that she really was done with me, and if she was, it would be no one's fault but mine.

Chapter Fifteen

Millie

Ashok waited for me when I arrived at the Bellariva Café, which was sandwiched between a salon offering eyebrow threading and a vintage clothing shop. He shoved the phone he'd been scrolling on into his pocket and stepped forward to greet me. With his dark suit, slicked-back hair and an iPad under his arm, he looked like every other letting agent I'd dealt with since I'd first started trying to find a suitable location to rent, but his handshake was firm rather than clammy and his smile seemed genuine.

"Miss Jeffers, nice to meet you. Is Mr Ferguson not with you?"

I'd almost forgotten that when I'd made the appointment to view the café, Kyle had intended to come along. Things had gone wrong between us so quickly, and I hadn't thought to inform the estate agency I'd be on my own.

"No, it's just me at the moment."

Ashok nodded. "No problem, no problem at all. Are you ready for the guided tour of the place?"

"Sure."

He unlocked the front door and launched into his spiel as he led me inside. "As you know, this café only came on the market within the last few days, but already we're getting a great deal of interest. I've already shown it to a couple of parties who seem very keen but to be honest, I'm not sure they have all the necessary finance in place."

I turned in a slow circle, casting a critical eye over the premises. I didn't know how recently the café had stopped trading, but everything had been left in good order. Chairs were stacked on the small wooden tables, the empty display shelves were clean and tidy, and the barista-style coffee machine on the back counter appeared brand new, its gleaming metal polished to a shine.

"You know, I wasn't entirely surprised to hear the Rinaldis had decided to retire," Ashok went on as I wandered through to the kitchen area, "only that they packed up and moved out as quickly as they did. But with their lease coming up for renewal, I suppose it made sense. And with them wanting to return to Naples…"

"So, you knew the old business quite well?" I paused in my inspection of the oven, pleased to note that it also appeared to be brand new. Already I was considering the practicalities of taking over the café – the number of staff I'd need to employ, the kind of menu customers would expect, the opening hours, and how I'd manage to run it on a day-to-day basis while still supplying

Sheila at Highgate Grounds with her regular order and fulfilling any postal orders for brownies and cupcakes.

"Our office is just around the corner. I often came in here for a cappuccino and one of their toasted ciabatta rolls." Ashok leaned back against the counter, his smile growing broader. "Everyone loved the Rinaldis. You would have never known that Enzo was nearly seventy, and Maria..."

I cut in before he could give me the family's entire life history. "Everything in the back looks as if it's been renovated fairly recently."

"Yes. The Rinaldis had complained that the oven was getting old and unreliable, so the landlord had the entire kitchen refitted. He likes to keep his tenants happy, particularly ones who'd been here for as long as they had."

Yeah, and I bet he could point to the renovations if he needed to justify increasing the rent...

I didn't say anything as I walked back into the main part of the café, still turning over the potential operating costs in my mind.

Ashok's voice floated from where he stood by the front window. "I can already tell you love this place, Miss Jeffers. And once you've put your own stamp on things..."

I ran my fingertips along the counter. They came away clean of dust and grease. "And what is this area like? I mean, I don't really know this part of the Holloway Road too well."

"Oh, I can tell you it's definitely on the up. Lots of interesting shops and offices around here, lots of people looking for coffee and something nice to eat. You said you're intending to sell cakes, right?" When I nodded, he went on, "Can't ever go wrong with a good piece of cake. Well, you'll notice on the literature you received from us that the building is licensed for Class E use, which allows you to sell cold food for consumption off the premises. That means you wouldn't need to apply for a change of use if you're operating as a shop as well as a café. And you're only a couple of minutes' walk away from Highbury Corner and the Overground station here, so you're practically in Islington."

I had to give him credit, he really had his patter down, and it might have been enough to convince me if I hadn't already decided I wanted this café. It wasn't too big, and the shiny new kitchen was a strong point in its favour. All it needed was a fresh coat of paint and some more modern furniture and I'd be good to go.

"How soon would I be able to move in?"

"As soon as you want. Though before you go ahead and sign the agreement, you'd have to meet the rental premium the landlord requires."

I looked at the listing I clutched in my hand again. The premium on any commercial property in this area wasn't going to come cheaply, and this was no exception. The landlord was effectively asking for forty thousand pounds as an upfront payment to secure the lease on the premises, and my heart sank. I didn't have that kind of money spare.

"Of course. This place is just perfect." I tried to keep my tone level. In my initial excitement, I hadn't really paid much attention to any costs other than the annual rent on the café and staff wages, which I hadn't foreseen too much difficulty meeting. I'd established my brownie business using the money from my redundancy pay-off, but by now that was all but gone. I could try to raise the forty thousand by taking out a business loan, or even by releasing some of the equity in my apartment, but I had no idea how long any of that would take. All I knew was by the time I had everything sorted out, someone else would have come along and snapped up the lease, leaving me back at the start of my property search.

Why did I take Kyle up on his offer to help me out with my finances? I should have just said no when he suggested it and forgotten about trying to open a shop. Though if we hadn't had that stupid falling-out about all the stuff I found in his bag, this wouldn't be a problem. But then I wouldn't know how he really earns his money and…

"Miss Jeffers?" Ashok's voice cut into my thoughts. "If you're really serious about taking on the running of the café, then we can go round to my office and complete all the paperwork now, but I do have someone else booked in for a viewing in an hour, and, well…"

I couldn't stall for time any longer. I'd have to tell him I was sorry, but as much as I loved the café, I didn't have the necessary finance to meet the landlord's premium and —

"Hey, Millie, sorry I'm late. The traffic on the Balls Pond Road was a nightmare."

I turned at the sound of Kyle's voice. He stood in the doorway, wearing the long charcoal-grey overcoat he'd had on the day I first met him by Highgate Grounds, smiling like we'd never exchanged a cross word.

"Kyle. You're here?" I tried and failed not to seem surprised.

"Yeah, just like I said I would be." He walked over to join me, looking around the room and smiling to himself as he appraised our surroundings. "This is really nice, Millie. I think this is the one."

The way he spoke, like he really was as invested in this project as me, made me want to wipe the infuriating little smirk off his face. I wanted to yell at him, ask him what the hell he thought he was doing here after everything, but I couldn't lose my cool with him in front of a virtual stranger. I had to make the estate agent think I was the right person to be taking over the lease of a thriving and popular establishment, not someone who would blow up at their so-called business partner in the middle of a viewing.

"I have to say, Mr Ferguson, you have a good eye for these things." Ashok's tone was pure flattery, and he stepped a little closer to Kyle, as if sensing he was the one who had real control of the finances. "As I told Miss Jeffers, all the important fixtures and fittings were recently upgraded, meaning a lot less work for you to do before you move in, and there's a lot of long-standing goodwill for this café in the local area. You're practically guaranteed returning customers from the day you reopen."

Kyle nodded as if this was what he'd been hoping to hear. "That all sounds very promising."

"When you arrived, Miss Jeffers and I had just reached the stage of discussing the rental premium on the property," Ashok went on.

"Which is?" Kyle asked.

"Forty thousand pounds," I told him, sure he would appreciate this wasn't a sum of money I had any hope of getting my hands on. I wanted this conversation to be over so Kyle could walk back out of my life.

"Well, that shouldn't be a problem. I assume the landlord will accept a bank transfer?"

It was the last thing I'd expected Kyle to say, and it left me confounded. I looked over at Ashok. "Excuse me. My…partner and I need to have a word."

"Of course."

I led Kyle out of the building. I didn't really want to have an argument with him in front of people passing by on the pavement, but neither did I want Ashok to hear what I was about to say.

"Kyle, what the hell do you think you're doing? You turn up here, all smiles, acting like you're a part of these negotiations, and blithely tell the letting agent you're going to pay the forty thousand pounds the landlord's asking for the privilege of renting the café… Well, I don't need your money."

He scoffed. "Obviously you do. Be serious, Millie, do you have that kind of cash to hand right now?" When I didn't answer, he continued, "I didn't think so. And I can see how badly you want this place, so why don't you let me do what I was going to, and act as your backer."

"Because I don't want to run a business that's paid for with drug money. And I don't want you to have any kind of financial hold over me."

Kyle took a step back and slapped a hand to his chest, as if my barb had wounded him. "Hey, you don't think the reason I'm doing this is because I want to and because I'd like to see you succeed?"

I put my fingers to my temples, where a slight headache had begun to throb. "Honestly, I don't know what to think. I thought we'd said we wouldn't see each other for a while. Maybe not ever again—"

"No, *you* said that. I hate being apart from you, and I don't want us to break up, Millie. I thought we had something really special."

"So did I." My voice was little more than a murmur. Being around Kyle stirred up so many conflicting emotions, and I couldn't deny that when he'd appeared in the café, suited and booted and with the faintest hint of a five o'clock shadow on his chin, my heart had skipped a beat. I hated how much I still wanted him, but whether I wanted to admit it or not, he affected me in a way no one else ever had.

I remembered what Emily had told me when we'd been talking in her staff room. *Bad people can have good hearts.* Didn't the fact that Kyle was here, wanting to help me out, prove that? Yet I still couldn't shake the nagging feeling that he saw his involvement in my business as a way of using me to launder his dirty money.

"I went to see my mum," he went on. "She...she's very close to the end now. I know she's trying to put a brave face on things for me, but I'm trying to prepare myself for the worst. And I started thinking there's nothing I can do to stop myself losing her, but I really don't want to lose you, too."

The slight glassiness to his eyes told me he was trying not to tear up, thinking about his mum. I laid a hand on his arm, wanting to comfort him even while I was still so angry with him for having lied to me about his criminal activities. I knew I should turn down his offer, but the moment I'd stepped inside the café, my only thought had been, *I want this place.* And without Kyle's involvement, that simply wasn't going to happen.

"If we do this" —I hesitated—"everything's going to be above the law, right?"

"Trust me, I would never do anything that would bring the police to your door." Kyle sounded so sincere that I pushed all my nagging doubts aside.

"So, if you lend me the forty thousand…"

"This isn't a loan, Millie. This is my gift to you." When I tried to argue, to tell him I intended to repay every penny he was giving me, he went on, "I've done a lot of bad things in my life, things I know you don't approve of. I want to prove to you that's not all I am. That's why I'm giving you this money with no strings attached."

"So, you'll be…what, my sleeping partner?" As soon as I'd said it, I knew Kyle would take my comment in a way I hadn't intended.

He smirked in response. I knew he had to be thinking, as I was, of the nights we'd spent together, tangled in the sheets of his bed, and mine. I shook my head, clearing it of the image.

"We're going to make this work," Kyle assured me. "Come on, let's go back inside."

He held the door open for me, and we went back to join Ashok, who shoved his phone in his pocket as we approached. I couldn't help wondering if he'd been checking on the other clients who he had lined up to view the café.

"Well?" He fixed us with his most professional smile.

"Miss Jeffers is happy for me to make the bank transfer to you to cover the premium on the property," Kyle told him. "And we have no other questions apart from how soon can we get this all sorted?"

"In which case, let's go to my office and we'll complete the paperwork."

Chapter Sixteen

Kyle

I'd thought Millie might show some emotion — happiness, relief even — as we left the letting agency office, but instead she seemed quiet and withdrawn.

"Is everything okay?" I asked her. "You're not having second thoughts about this, are you?"

She shook her head as she turned to me. "No, I'm sure I've made the right decision, but I guess it's all taking a little while to sink in. I mean, the Bellariva Café is mine now, and... Kyle, I have so much to do before I can even think about opening for customers. I've got to find someone to help me out behind the counter and in the kitchen, I need to set up social media profiles to make sure everyone knows the place is under new management, find out what information I need to give to the local council and whoever supplies the utilities —"

"Hey, don't worry about it. You did your homework before you began looking for somewhere to rent. I'm sure you have a lot of that in hand already. And, like I said, I'll help you out wherever I can, seeing as we're partners in this venture."

She gave me a half-smile, but there was a wariness in her eyes. I could tell some small part of her wished she hadn't accepted my help, but Millie was pragmatic. Without my financial contribution, she'd still be packing up brownie orders on her kitchen table. Now, she'd have the regular clientele and the cosy café she'd dreamed of, and I really wanted her to make a success of it all.

"You know what we need to do before any of that?" When she looked at me blankly, I went on, "Celebrate!"

"Oh, I don't know if I should." She hesitated, glancing back at the café as if still thinking of all the work she needed to do to get it up and running as soon as possible.

"Come on, you deserve it. I bet when you got that fancy financial job of yours, you had a drink or two to mark the occasion, right?"

Millie nodded, recalling the occasion. "My flatmate at the time and I went to this wine bar near Cannon Street and shared a bottle of the cheapest red on the menu. Which still cost more than I'd ever spent on a single bottle in my life up until that point. And I remember this awful City type with greased-back hair and red braces and an inflated opinion of himself trying to chat us up. You know that film *The Wolf of Wall Street*? Well, Sarah, my flatmate, called this guy the mangy old tom cat of Wall Street, and we started laughing so hard I thought they were going to ask us to leave." Her face brightened. "Okay, yes, why not?"

"Great. Come on, my car's parked just over there." I pointed to where I'd grabbed the last available parking bay on the block, conscious that the time I'd paid for was almost up.

We hurried over and I got in the car. I moved a couple of boxes off the passenger seat and into the back so Millie could sit beside me. If she wondered what I might be storing in those boxes, she didn't say anything.

"Right, let's go," I said half to myself as we pulled away from the kerb. I had no idea where to take her—an occasion like this demanded something a little nicer than one of the backstreet pubs I might otherwise have chosen—but as we drove down Upper Street and the Business Design Centre loomed up ahead, I had an idea. A few hotels had sprung up in the area, mostly aimed at the people who came here for conferences. Any one of them would have a halfway decent bar with discreet service, which was exactly what we needed right now.

The underground carpark near Islington Green was almost full, but I managed to find a spot between a sleek silver people carrier and a cream-coloured Mini Cooper. When we emerged onto the forecourt of the Design Centre, I noticed a sign welcoming visitors to the North London Student Careers Fair, and a line of people at the main entrance, waiting to get in.

I hurried Millie past the snaking queue and led her towards the modern-looking hotel ahead of us. Large floor-to-ceiling glass windows gave a view into a bar with low cream sofas and subdued lighting. It was barely midday, but a pair of guests sitting at a table with pint glasses in front of them reassured me the place was serving alcohol.

"Do we have to be guests here to get a drink?" Millie asked as we breezed through the reception area and followed the signs for the bar and restaurant.

"Don't you worry about that," I told her. I found us seats in a quiet corner, well away from the window, then went to the bar.

"Good day, sir. What can I get you?" The barman had white-blond hair and an accent that marked him as coming from somewhere in Eastern Europe.

"A bottle of rosé champagne and two glasses, please."

He didn't ask for my room number, which I took as a good sign. I waited while he opened the champagne, twisting the cork so delicately it came out with a sigh rather than a pop, and placed it in an ice bucket. I tapped the pre-paid card against the reader, stuffed the receipt the barman gave me into my pocket, then carried the bucket and the two glasses over to Millie.

She raised an eyebrow as I shrugged off my coat, took a seat on the overstuffed sofa next to her and poured her drink. "Pink champagne?"

I shrugged. "I thought it kind of suited the vibe." With a smile, I raised my glass. "Here's to you, Millie, and to the Bellariva Café becoming the success you deserve it to be."

"Thank you." She clinked her champagne flute against mine and took a sip. "Oh, this is lovely. A little of this and I could completely forget how much work I've got to do. Or was that your idea in bringing me here?"

I held up my hands, as if she'd caught me. "Guilty as charged, m'lady."

She gazed at her drink, watching the bubbles rise in steady streams towards the top of the glass. "When I first started selling cakes online, someone sent me an email and asked me whether they could get some champagne cupcakes — they wanted them for a bridal shower they were organising. Well, I made them as a one-off, and I used prosecco because it was a fraction of the price and when you're cooking with it, you really can't tell the difference. But I was pleased with how they turned out, and so was the client. And now I'm thinking, make them with pink champagne... I bet they'd go down well at weddings."

"Yeah, I can see Cameron and Emily wanting something like that."

She shot me a look. "They're getting married?"

"Not as far as I know, but the way he looks at her, like there's nothing more precious on earth, I doubt it'll be too long. And I wouldn't be surprised if Lynda keeps dropping hints about how she'd love Cameron to give her grandchildren like his brothers have. She strikes me as the type."

"Doesn't she just?" Millie muttered.

My flute was already half empty, and I reached to top it up.

"Is that a good idea," she asked me, "given that you're driving?"

"This will be my last glass," I assured her. "And it's not like there's anywhere I have to be for a while. We can just sit here, watch the world go by..."

I threw my arm along the back of the sofa. As if she wasn't aware of what she was doing, Millie leaned in a little closer to me. Testing the water, I dropped the fingertips of my free hand onto her shoulder. I figured if she didn't want the contact, she would move away, but she stayed where she was. She wore the perfume I'd come to associate with her, the one that smelled of freshly cut flowers and long summer days, and I longed to press my nose to her neck. A bolt of lust arrowed through me, straight to my crotch. My cock swelled, and I draped my coat over my lap so Millie wouldn't notice how excited she'd got me simply by snuggling up to me.

"I've missed this," she admitted, gazing off somewhere into the middle distance. "Missed being with you."

"I feel the same way." It was no lie. Every night since Millie had kicked me out of her apartment, I'd laid in bed and replayed our argument over and over. I'd broken her trust—broken her heart, too—and I'd do anything to get our relationship back to how it used to be. I didn't see how that could happen right now, but her being here with me, quietly sipping her champagne, was a small step on the path to becoming friends once more.

Slow down, man, you're reading far too much into this, I warned myself. *Maybe she's only doing this to be polite. You have just put up a big chunk of money on her behalf, after all...*

Her next words made me realise her thoughts were running along the same track as mine. "Do you ever wish you'd done something different, stopped things from turning out the way they did?"

Without thinking, I blurted out, "Yeah, I'd have made damn sure you didn't get to look inside my backpack."

She turned her head and stared at me, and for a moment I thought I'd blown it. I expected her to snatch up her coat and bag and storm out of the hotel bar, leaving me with the bottle of champagne and my insistent hard-on.

"Well, if you speak to my mother, she'd tell you I got what I deserved for snooping."

"You told your mother what happened?"

Millie giggled and took a big drink of her champagne before holding out her glass so I could refill it. "No way. If I had, she'd have been on the next train south out of Manchester Piccadilly so she could drag me back home, away from a bad influence like you."

"You think I'm a bad influence?" I looked at her through heavy-lidded eyes, giving up any pretence that we weren't flirting with each other.

"And if I do?"

"Then I'll have to find some way of proving to you that I'm not. Or maybe I should simply spank the notion out of you." I had no idea where the thought came from, but now it was front and centre in my imagination. Millie lying on my lap, her bare bottom upturned and blushing a delicious pink while I peppered it with slaps. My cock surged even more powerfully than before and I knew I had to think about something, anything else before I was completely lost.

Millie drained her glass in one big swallow, then poured herself some more and finished that, too. Before I had time to react, she had turned and taken my face between her hands. Her lips came down on mine, soft and wet, and I let out a surprised moan into her mouth. She kissed me, all but tumbling into my lap in her eagerness to press her body against mine.

When she finally broke the embrace, I looked around, glad the other customers in the bar were sitting at tables near the windows and weren't paying us the least bit of attention. Not that I hadn't enjoyed being smooched so thoroughly by her, but still, I had to ask. "Are...are we really doing this?"

"What, you don't want to kiss me?" Millie sounded offended and confused. I couldn't blame her, not if she'd got the impression my body was telling her one thing and my words another.

"Oh, I absolutely do want to. I meant here, in the middle of the bar. Because if you keep kissing and touching me, I can't guarantee I'm not going to rip your clothes off and fuck you on this sofa, with everyone in the room watching."

Her face flushed, like I'd triggered some secret fantasy of hers. Having sex in front of interested voyeurs had never appealed to me, but I couldn't help wondering what it would be like to fuck Millie for the benefit of an audience.

What if it's the Fox brothers? All three of them, getting off on watching me and Millie? Wanting what they can never have?

I decided against sharing that thought with Millie, but I knew I had to find out where we stood before she had second thoughts about going further with me.

"What we're doing, you and me… I just need to know that we're not making a mistake."

Millie didn't hesitate in her answer. "If we are, it'll be the best mistake we ever made."

"Good. As long as you're okay with this."

"Believe me. I'm more than okay. So, what are we going to do about it?" she asked.

I knocked back the last of my champagne. She eyed the empty glass, clearly calculating in her head how much we'd both had to drink and how I was more than likely over the safe driving limit. "Well, we need a place with a big, comfortable bed, where we can take our time. Luckily, we're somewhere that's full of them." I got to my feet and held out a hand to her. "Come on, Millie, let's treat ourselves to a room."

Chapter Seventeen

Millie

Kyle went up to the front desk and waited until the clerk had finished with whatever she was doing on the computer screen in front of her. He tapped his fingers against his thigh, barely able to contain his impatience. When she finally glanced up, he treated her to his most dazzling smile.

"Good afternoon, sir. How can I help you?" Her tone was clipped, her accent faintly South African, and her blonde hair was twisted into a bun so tight I was convinced it must give her a constant headache.

"We'd like a double room, please."

"Of course." She tapped her keyboard. "Standard or superior?"

"Whatever you have available." He fidgeted, clearly not wanting to have this conversation. I'd already learned that when Kyle was set on a plan, he wanted to put it into action as quickly as possible.

"Well, the superior comes with the king-sized bed…"

Kyle turned and gave me a saucy little wink. I had to smother the giggle that rose to my lips. He returned his attention to the desk clerk. "Yes, that would suit us nicely."

"Very good, sir. That's a superior room for two." She typed something in, then looked up at him again. "With breakfast?"

"Oh, I don't think we'll still be here at breakfast time," Kyle informed her.

"So, you'd like an early checkout?"

"No, I mean we're only going to need the room for the next couple of hours."

She looked at him as if he'd said he wanted to rampage through the lobby on the back of an elephant. "I'm afraid that won't be possible. Our room rates are strictly for overnight stays."

"Right, whatever. In which case, I'll pay for the night but that doesn't mean I'll be here all night, if that's okay with you?"

The desk clerk set her lips in a tight line. I could tell she was fighting the urge to ask Kyle and me to leave at once. She tapped her keyboard again. "May I take your name?"

"Smith," Kyle shot back. "I'm Mr Smith and this is Mrs Smith."

I caught Kyle's gaze. He winked at me, and I bit my tongue. He couldn't have chosen a cornier fake name and we both knew it, but this was all part of the fantasy. I remembered Amanda telling me about a weekend she and Jim had spent in Brighton. They'd checked in to a hotel on the seafront, then gone down to the bar separately and acted like two strangers flirting over a drink. She'd said the sex they'd had when they'd finally gone up to their room, still pretending they'd never met before that night, had been some of the hottest of their marriage. I'd never dreamed I might find myself doing a similar thing.

"All right...Mr Smith." The desk clerk's tone made it clear that she was barely tolerating Kyle's little game. "You'll be in room two-one-four on the second floor. And that will be one hundred and eighty pounds for the night."

Kyle opened his wallet and counted out twenty-pound notes with a flourish, as if the amount of money was of no consequence. I waited while they completed the checking-in process, listening to the soft piped music and trying to stop my mind racing ahead to the moment when Kyle and I would be alone.

"So, here's your key card," the clerk said. "And the lifts are over there to your right. Enjoy your stay...Mr Smith...Mrs Smith."

"Thank you, we intend to." Kyle put his arm around me and guided me in the direction of the bank of lifts. Somehow, he managed to keep his hands off me till we got to our room, but as soon as the door was firmly shut behind us, he tossed the coat he'd been carrying aside and pushed me down onto the big bed.

"King-sized, just like that snooty woman on reception promised," he murmured.

I gazed up at him from where I lay sprawled on the bland chocolate and white covers. "I'm sure she was only doing her job."

"Yeah, but the way she was looking at me, like she had a bad smell under her nose the whole time..." His tone gave me the impression he wasn't used to women treating him with such disdain, especially not ones who spent most of the day behind a desk dealing with customers.

"I suppose a place like this, set up for exhibition guests, maybe they don't get many people who want a room so they can get up to something naughty," I suggested. "Or maybe not many who are quite as brazen about it as you were."

"Exhibition guests?" Kyle snorted. "They're the worst. They're like people who go to sales conferences and trade shows. Away from their regular partners for a day or two, off the leash, surrounded by attractive strangers. Trust me, all half of them want to do is drink, take drugs, have freaky sex with someone they'll never see again…"

Distaste must have crossed my face when he mentioned drugs. It wouldn't surprise me if the reason he knew so much about all this was because he'd been the person who supplied them. Before I could dwell on the thought, Kyle rolled onto the bed next to me and swept me up in an embrace.

The soft press of his mouth against mine swept aside any thoughts of his illegal activities. I twined my fingers in his hair as we picked up where we'd left off in the hotel bar. Our kisses grew hotter, more passionate, as I nipped at Kyle's lower lip, and he snaked a hand down to cup my breast through the tailored black top I'd worn to our meeting with the letting agent.

"You taste so good," he murmured. He dragged his lips down the side of my neck. The slight prick of his stubble had me shivering and longing for him to move his mouth even lower, where I was already wet with need for him.

"What you were saying in the bar," I said between kisses, "about ripping my clothes off and fucking me…"

He paused in what he was doing so he could stare down at me, his pupils blown wide with lust. "Yeah?"

"Maybe don't rip anything — this outfit was kind of expensive — but I'm ready for the fucking part."

"You are, huh?" As he spoke, he tugged at the zip on my skirt and pulled it down. His smile broadened at the sight of the flimsy panties and lace-topped hold-up stockings I wore underneath it — underwear I'd worn to give me the confidence I needed for my meeting with the letting agent. Kyle put his fingers between my legs, pressing the crotch of my underwear against my sensitive clit, and I shuddered at his touch. He gave a small nod. "Yeah, I'd say that's ready."

I raised myself up on my elbows. "So, what are you waiting for?"

"Only this." Kyle brought his wallet out of his trouser pocket and glanced into it. A frown creased his brow. "I thought I had condoms in here, but — "

"Don't worry about it. Toss me my handbag, would you?"

He did as I asked. Buried deep in the bag, along with a packet of tissues, lipsticks in varying shades and a roll of soft mints, was my emergency kit. Amanda had given it to me weeks ago, when she'd found out how serious things were getting between me and Kyle.

"Just in case you find yourself staying the night with him," she'd said. "It won't prevent you having to do the walk of shame entirely, but it'll make some things easier." The kit, contained in a soft green zip-up purse, consisted of a couple of tampons, paracetamol tablets, plasters, lip balm, a hair tie and — I smiled to myself as I fished them out — a strip of condoms.

Kyle tore off one of the foil packages and handed the rest back to me. He laid it on the bedside table in my eyeline, like a promise of what was to come.

When he kissed me again, his mouth devoured mine, hungry and urgent, like he wanted to make up for all the time we'd spent apart. He swallowed down my sighs as I traced my hands over the firm line of his jaw and down his neck.

He broke away to pull the tie loose from his collar. He seemed about to toss it aside, then something occurred to him. He stroked the length of black fabric, regarding me with a hungry gaze. "Millie, have you ever been tied up?"

"What? No, I…" Whatever I'd been expecting him to suggest, it hadn't been this.

"Okay, but have you ever wanted to?"

"Honestly? Well, the thought of it excites me, but…" When I glanced up at him, he seemed to be on tenterhooks, waiting for my response. "I guess I've just never been with anyone I trusted enough to play that kind of game with. I've had a few boyfriends, but none of them had what you'd call a dominant streak."

"And you trust me?" The uncertainty in his tone had me biting my lip. His confidence melted away for an instant, showing me the vulnerable side of him he did his best to hide. "God knows I haven't given you many reasons to."

"If I didn't, I wouldn't be here now." I said it as much to convince myself as him. The discovery of his drug dealing had shaken me, enough that I'd been determined to break up with him — for good, or so I'd thought. But seeing him again today had made me realise how much I still wanted him. I'd told myself I couldn't live with him but now I knew I couldn't live without him. "And if I thought you intended to hurt me, I would never have come up to the room with you in the first place."

Now his expression seemed genuinely wounded. "Hurt you? Oh, Millie, that's the last thing I'd ever do to you. But if you're at all concerned, then we won't do this."

He was about to drop his tie to the floor, but I stopped him. I knew how important it was for him to hear me voice my desires and to know I consented to be his. "Do it, Kyle. Tie me to the bed. Make my desires come true."

"Okay, but first these have to come off." He pulled my top over my head, then unsnapped the fastening of my bra and added that to the rapidly growing pile of clothes on the floor. I trembled as he gazed at me. He'd only removed his tie, and the contrast between my half-naked body and his smart suit helped to establish the power balance between us in this game. He was the master, and I was his submissive plaything, just as I dreamed in those kinky fantasies that I kept a secret between me and my vibrator.

Kyle took a moment to remove his shoes and suit jacket. I longed for him to strip out of the rest of his clothes, but I knew I didn't have a say in when that happened. Never breaking eye contact with me, he took his tie and wound it around my wrists, fastening them together.

The bed had a padded headboard, and surrounding it, a black metal rail, with just enough of a gap between the two to make me think whoever designed the room might have had this kind of sex game in mind. Kyle fastened the loose ends of the tie around the rail and secured them with a sloppy knot. I gave my makeshift bondage a tug, trying to work out how easy it would be to wriggle free if I needed to. I reckoned it wouldn't take too much effort on my part, but I was sure that he would loosen my bonds at once if I appeared to be in any kind of distress.

Kyle regarded me for a long moment, clearly liking the way my body looked so blatantly displayed and with my hands tied to the bedrail. "You've never done anything like this before, and neither have I, but I know enough about bondage to be clear that you need a safe word. Something to let me know you're not enjoying yourself and you want me to stop."

It was something I'd never needed to consider before today, and I racked my brain for a suitable word. My gaze fell on the arty black-and-white photo of the London skyline hanging on the opposite wall. The biggest and most prominent of the skyscrapers drew my attention. "How about 'Shard'?"

He nodded. "That works for me. Okay, so now I have you exactly where I want you…"

He crouched over me and cupped my pussy through the wet crotch of my panties. The firm pressure of his fingers against my clit, barely softened by the thin strip of cotton and lace, had me shuddering against the bedcovers.

"I guess it wouldn't take much to make you come, right?" The teasing tone in his voice let me know he was considering all the possibilities of how he could enjoy bringing me off, and I nodded, eager for him to touch me where I needed it the most. He smirked as he pulled his hand away, making me whimper in disappointment. "But I'm not going to do that just yet. Maybe I won't do it at all." He put his fingers back where they'd been, pressing a little harder this time. "Maybe I should just keep taking you right to the brink but never allow you to go over it. After all, you look so cute right now, all horny and frustrated."

"Please..." I murmured, all too conscious that he was in charge here and nothing would happen unless he decided it should.

He tipped his head to the side and stared at me. "Please what?"

"Please...sir." I used the word that sprung to my lips in all the fantasies I'd had about Kyle. It seemed whether I cared to admit it or not, I'd been longing for him to take control in the bedroom.

"That's better." He slipped his hand down the front of my underwear and skimmed a fingertip between my pussy lips. I bit my lip as he skirted over my clit, treating it to the lightest of touches before he withdrew again.

He hadn't been lying when he said he wanted to keep me on edge. My nerves were frazzled, my body aching for him to give me what I craved, but I was certain that the more I begged, the more he'd be inclined to carry out his threat of leaving me unsatisfied.

When I was starting to think I couldn't take any more of this devilish torment, he grasped the waistband of my panties and pulled them down. Once he had them off, he used the flats of his palms to push my thighs wide apart. He held me like that for a long moment, open and bared to him, drinking in the sight of me. His intense scrutiny should have made me uncomfortable, but I could see in his eyes how beautiful he found me.

"This seems like the right moment to remind myself of how you taste." He shifted on the bed, getting down so his head was between my legs. His warm, wet mouth settling over my pussy had me squealing with joy and he stopped what he was doing. When he fixed his gaze on me, his expression was severe. "Millie, please. There may be people in the neighbouring room, and I'm sure they don't want to be disturbed. Maybe I should gag you with your underwear to stop you making all that noise?"

"No, please." I didn't know whether he was joking, but I could easily see him wadding my panties into a ball and stuffing them into my mouth.

"In which case, do you promise to be quiet?"

"Yes, I do, sir."

"Good. Though I'll warn you now. If you break your promise and I hear anyone knock on the door, I will let them in. I don't care whether it's another guest here to complain or housekeeping wanting to clean our room, they're coming inside. And what will they think when they see you spread out on the bed naked with your hands tied to the bedrail?"

Even as I told myself he would never do anything like this, I couldn't help imagining the door bursting open and a curious maid or angry neighbour walking in to find me helpless and at Kyle's mercy. I turned my head away so Kyle wouldn't see the confusion and want I was sure must be emblazoned across my face.

"So, be a good girl and keep it down for me, okay?" He put his finger to my lips as I nodded my agreement.

When his tongue swiped over my wet sex, it took everything I had not to yell out in pleasure. He knew just what to do to have me squirming beneath him, frantic for more. Fast little licks, like a cat lapping up cream, broken up with long, slow sweeps all the way down to my rear hole. I spread my legs further, wishing I had my hands free so I could grab his head and hold it in place while he pleasured me.

When he raised his head to glance at me, his gaze was feral, possessive. My juices shone on his chin. The bland scent of whatever products the cleaning staff used to freshen the air in the room had been replaced by the strong aroma of sex as we both grew more excited.

I needed him to put his mouth back where it had been, but instead he reached out to snag the condom from where it lay on the table beside the bed. He took his time undressing, clearly aware of how badly I needed to be fucked but wanting to remind me he still had the power in this situation.

At long last, he rolled the condom over his erection. He held my legs wide apart and eased into me with one slow, assured stroke. My cry of pleasure as he filled me to the brim was muted as I remembered his threats of what he'd do if I was too noisy, but it seemed like Kyle didn't care about that any longer. He grunted as he started to thrust, pushing in as far as he could before pulling back out almost all the way.

"I wish this didn't feel so good," I murmured. "Then it would have been easier to let you go."

"We're meant to be together." Kyle's words were punctuated by emphatic jerks of his hips. "You might want to pretend that's not the case, but we both know it."

He was right. However much I tried to deny it, my world was smaller, less interesting when he wasn't in it. I'd thought I could manage without him, but deep down, I responded to him in a way I never had with anyone else. And when he stared into my eyes, I was sure he felt the same.

The luxurious mattress barely moved beneath us as Kyle quickened the pace of his fucking. Unable to grip him with my hands, I locked my ankles together around his back. In this position, he seemed to push even deeper into me. I cried out his name as he hit the spot that made me come undone.

As the walls of my pussy squeezed hard around him and I floated in a world of bliss, Kyle shuddered and came. We stayed locked together for a moment before he sighed and, with obvious reluctance, pulled out of me.

He tugged at the tie he'd used to fasten me in place, and I stretched out my arms and rolled my shoulders to ease the slight ache that had built there.

"I'm going to take a shower," I told him.

"Give me a minute and I'll join you." He glanced at the time on his phone screen. "Though there's no need to hurry. We have got this room all night, if we want it." He half sat up. "What do you say? After we've showered, we could order some room service, maybe get some more champagne, then I can fuck your brains out all over again."

I lingered in the doorway leading to the en suite bathroom. "Sounds like you've got this all figured out."

"Trust me, Millie. I always have."

As I turned on the shower, I heard him speaking to someone on his phone. I caught the words 'two-one-four' and presumed he was ordering food for both of us.

So, I guess this means we're officially back together.

I glanced at my reflection as I waited for the water to heat. So much for my efforts to get Kyle Ferguson out of my life. But if I were being honest, I had to admit it was so much nicer having him back in it. He'd promised he would keep his dealing well away from the café, and I'd done my best to draw the lines I wouldn't allow him to cross. I only hoped I could live with the consequences.

Chapter Eighteen

Millie

Signing the lease to the Bellariva Café was the easy bit. The hard work started once I was back home after Kyle and I finally left the hotel, and I found myself sitting at the kitchen table, staring at the never-ending list of the things that needed to be done before I could officially open at the end of the month.

Completing all the paperwork I'd mentioned to Kyle stood at the top of the list, with phone numbers and website addresses for the local council and the various utility companies scrawled alongside them. Once I'd got all the tedious bureaucracy out of the way, I could start thinking about the changes that would make the place look and feel my own. My tenancy might come with the majority of the fixtures and fittings intact — most importantly, the shiny new oven and walk-in refrigerators that would make working in the kitchen a dream — but the décor was overdue a serious refresh. I needed stocks of everything from plates and mugs to bulk bags of coffee beans and paper cartons for boxing up orders when customers popped in for cakes to take away. Not to mention I needed to find someone to help me with the cooking and maybe another member of staff to take orders and man the bakery counter.

My phone buzzed with a text as I returned to the table with a fresh cup of coffee and a couple of chocolate digestives.

Hey, you left these in the car.

Kyle had added a pair of glove emojis to the message. A second text swiftly followed.

Want me to drop them off now?

Tempting as it was to have Kyle pay me a visit, the list I'd been compiling nagged at me. I tapped out a quick reply.

I'll pick them up the next time I see you. Too much to do right now…

He sent back a disappointed face, followed by *Let me know how I can help.*

"You could send a team of magic elves to help me get the café in order," I murmured to myself. I still had doubts over letting Kyle get involved in my business, but now I'd allowed him to put up the money, I had to make this work.

Still half-joking, I texted him back.

If you know somewhere I can get a load of latte glasses cheaply, I'll love you forever.

I didn't expect to hear back from him, but within seconds, he responded.

There's a kitchen supply store on the big industrial estate up the road from the café. You can get your gloves from me when I take you there.

The speed with which he'd got back to me was impressive. Was he already aware of the place, or had he Googled it on my behalf? Either way, it was good to get the feeling he wanted to help me out. Maybe he was taking his role as a silent partner in my business more seriously than I'd expected. I only hoped this was an omen of good things to come.

* * * *

Kyle was as good as his word. Two days later, he drove me up to the Archway branch of Robertsons Catering Supplies so I could get everything I thought I'd need. The list I'd put together after browsing their website seemed never-ending—I couldn't believe I'd forgotten about disposable coffee cups for takeaway orders, even though I hoped to encourage customers to bring their own and cut down on waste. Still, Kyle helped me pick out what I wanted, load everything into the back of his car, and sign my business up to the trade customers scheme that would earn me ten percent off future purchases.

If that wasn't enough, to save me having to pay for a professional decorator, Kyle met me at the café one morning armed with several cans of magnolia paint and set about applying a fresh coat to the walls. Of course, despite his best efforts, he managed to get drips of paint across his cheeks and in his hair, and removing them involved a long, steamy shower in his bathroom, with me massaging creamy lather into his skin before we ended up having noisy sex on his big, comfortable bed.

His efforts at DIY were more than worth it. The soothing colour scheme, coupled with hanging ceiling lights that gave off a soft yellow glow and plant shelves on each wall, filled with a selection of spider plants and long-leafed ferns in terracotta pots, gave the place the kind of feel I wanted to create. It wasn't so buzzy and modern that it would alienate the Bellariva's old clientele, but I hoped it would attract people who wanted to take their time enjoying coffee and a brownie.

The morning when I finally threw open the café's doors for business, I was a bag of nerves. I'd barely slept a wink the night before, convinced it was going to be a disaster, and I wouldn't have a single customer. Despite my fears, I'd barely finished putting the last of the freshly baked goods on the shelves when an old woman wandered in, took a seat at the table in the window and asked for a mug of tea and a toasted teacake.

Jasmine, who I'd employed as my assistant manager pretty much straight out of catering college and who seemed determined to repay my faith in her by being efficient and dependable, took her order over when it was ready. The woman poured a little milk into her tea and sipped it. I held my breath as she stared over the rim of her mug for a moment, then announced, "Not bad, love. Not bad at all." I wasn't sure whether she was referring to her drink or to the café as a whole, but her considered praise meant everything to me.

The old woman was followed by a couple of mothers with prams wanting hot chocolate with cream and marshmallows to take away, then a girl who bought a box of mixed cupcakes from the selection on display, and as a queue began to form at the bakery counter, I couldn't suppress the smile of satisfaction creeping across my face.

A line I recalled from one of my mum's favourite films drifted into my head.

If you build it, they will come.

The bell over the door jangled again as more people walked in, and I glanced around the busy café. I hadn't just built my dream, I had poured my heart and soul into it, and now the customers were coming. I'd put my doubts about Kyle behind me, and he had encouraged me every step of the way to this moment. I really didn't think things could get any better.

Chapter Nineteen

Millie

"Hey, stranger!" The voice echoed across the café, distracting me from the brownies I was packaging up for one of my regular customers.

I looked up to see Amanda, in a chic camel trench coat and houndstooth-check suit, walking towards the counter. I turned to Jasmine. "Would you mind completing the payment for this one?"

"Sure." Jasmine took the box from me, and I went over to greet Amanda.

"What are you doing here?" I asked.

"Don't sound so surprised to see me, honey. I told you I'd stop by when I had the chance, and I just finished up a meeting with a new client who's based at Highbury Corner, so…here I am. Ready for someone to take my order."

"Okay, what'll you have?"

She tapped her immaculately manicured index finger against her lip as she studied the drinks board behind the counter. "A large skinny cappuccino with an extra shot to go, and one of those nice-looking blueberry scones, no butter."

"Coming right up."

In the last couple of weeks, I'd become a wizard on the espresso machine. I ground the beans and tamped them in the filter, aware of Amanda leaning on the counter to watch. I knew how fussy she was about the coffee she bought—more than once I'd seen her take her drink back to the barista and ask them to make it again if it wasn't to her exact taste.

"No pressure," I muttered to myself as I foamed the milk and poured the coffee into a tall disposable cup. I pressed the lid on tight, slipped a paper collar around the cup so it wouldn't be too hot to hold and passed it to Amanda, along with the scone she'd asked for.

"Thanks, Millie. What do I owe you?"

I waved the question away. "This is on me. To say thank you for being such a great friend."

"Oh, no." Her head shake was emphatic as she brandished her platinum credit card. "I insist. I've carried out too many audits not to know that giving things away is the quickest way to go out of business." She waited for me to bring over the payment terminal, then tapped her card against it. Once I'd handed her the receipt, she tasted her drink. I crossed my fingers behind my back, hoping it met her high standards.

"Okay?" I asked, doing my best to sound like it wouldn't wound me to the core if she didn't like it.

"Perfect. I'll be coming back here, and next time I'll bring Jim with me."

"Bring a reusable cup, too. That way you'll get twenty-five pence off your coffee — and I do know how much you love a bargain."

She dropped the paper bag containing her scone into her roomy shoulder bag. "So, now we've got that out of the way, how are things between you and lover boy?"

I glanced over as the bell over the door tinkled. "Well, you can ask him yourself because here he is now."

Kyle strode up to the counter, a newspaper tucked under his arm. "Hey, Millie, can I get an Americano with just a splash of milk?" He jerked a thumb at the empty table by the wall. "I'll be sitting over there."

"Of course, but before you sit down, can I introduce you to Amanda?"

He turned and treated her to the full force of his charm. "Oh, so you're the famous Amanda I've heard so much about. How do you like Millie's little café, then?"

"It's so cute, and the coffee is to die for," Amanda gushed. "You must be so proud of her."

"I am, believe me. And now I'm going to sit at that table and read my paper while you two talk about me."

"Oh, honey, do you really think we're so predictable?" Amanda sounded like she didn't expect Kyle to answer. He winked at her and went to sit down.

I poured a little milk into his coffee and took it over to him. "I didn't expect to see you today."

"Well, I was at a loose end, so I thought, why not come over here and chill? Keep an eye on how my investment is going, you know."

I put a hand on my hip. "So, you're simply here on business, huh?"

He flicked his paper open and spread it out on the table in front of him. "That and keeping up to date with world news."

Amanda still leaned against the counter, watching the two of us with a rapt expression. "I'll leave you to it, then," I told him and returned to her.

"So, do you have any gossip for me?" I asked her, checking the clock and realising I had another couple of minutes before the batch of vanilla cupcakes baking in the oven were done.

She gave a dramatic sigh. "Oh, I'm sure you don't want to hear about all the boring office politics you left behind to— Hello, who's *that*?"

I followed the direction of Amanda's gaze to where Cameron Fox had pushed open the café door. "Trouble," I blurted without thinking. When she gave me a quizzical look, I corrected myself. "It's Cameron Fox. He's Kyle's half-brother, though what he's doing here—"

Amanda licked the foam from her cappuccino off her bottom lip as she watched Cameron stroll over to where Kyle sat. "Well, girlfriend, he is one fine-looking specimen. You didn't tell me all the men in that family were so hot."

"Hey, what would Jim say if he heard you talking like this?"

"Oh, Jim and I have an arrangement. We each have one person we'd be allowed to stray out of the confines of holy matrimony for." She must have known she'd piqued my interest because she went on, "In his case, it's Scarlett Johansson, so it's not like he's ever going to have the opportunity."

"And who is yours?"

"To tell you the truth, even though we've talked about it, I've never seen anyone I'd seriously consider cheating on Jim with, but this guy?" She fanned herself with her fingers, as if it were suddenly too hot in the room. "He'd get it."

I was about to start listing off all the reasons why that would be the worst choice Amanda could ever make, but a young woman was wheeling her baby buggy over to the counter and Jasmine had disappeared into the kitchen—I assumed to check on the cupcakes. "Sorry, I need to serve this customer, but I'll be back. Just don't make any plans involving Cameron Fox. Trust me, it's not a good idea."

Amanda patted my arm. "Don't worry. I should have been back at the office ten minutes ago anyway. But I'll give you a ring later and we can catch up then."

"Thanks for coming in."

"Any time, honey." With that, she breezed out of the café.

I glanced over to where Cameron and Kyle sat in animated discussion. I didn't know what Cameron was doing here, and I suspected, if I found out, I wasn't going to like it. Had Kyle arranged to meet him in the café and decided against telling me, or was this purely a chance encounter? I tried not to think about it as I went to serve the woman with the buggy, but I couldn't help feeling like Cameron's sudden appearance had darkened what had been a good day until now.

Chapter Twenty

Kyle

"I thought I'd find you here."

I looked up from the copy of the *Metro* I'd been leafing through and met Cameron Fox's clear-eyed stare.

"You don't mind if I join you?" He pulled out a chair without waiting for my reply and plonked himself down opposite me.

I folded up my newspaper, knowing I wasn't about to get the chance to finish reading the story about the Chelsea manager's latest bust-up with his star striker.

Cameron glanced around the café. "Nice place," he commented. "Your girlfriend's done well for herself." He turned his head in the direction of the counter and waved a hand at Millie where she was still deep in conversation with Amanda. "Hey, Millie, sweetheart. Bring me a cup of tea when you have a moment, will you? And I want it strong enough to stand the spoon up in, and just the tiniest bit of milk, thanks."

A woman on the neighbouring table glanced at Cameron. Her lips were pursed, and I was sure she was about to tell him off for ruining the café's peaceful atmosphere, then she seemed to get a better look at him and her expression softened. When you were as handsome as any of the Fox brothers, you could pretty much get away with the worst behaviour. I guessed Cameron could whip out a lighter and set fire to the menu on the table we sat at, and the North London yummy mummies surrounding us would keep sipping their coffees and gossiping about how cute he was.

"So, what can I do for you?" I did my best to seem indifferent to Cameron's presence, but I couldn't help wondering why he'd sought me out. "I'm guessing you haven't come to invite me to Sunday lunch again."

"We need your help."

It was the last thing I'd expected from him. "I'm sorry?"

He gave a choked-off, disbelieving laugh. "Believe me, I'm as surprised to hear myself say that as you are. But, seriously, you want to be a proper part of our family, right?"

I nodded, wondering where he was going with this. "More than anything."

"Well, this is your in." My bafflement must have shown in my expression because Cameron continued, "Do what we're asking, and we'll know without a doubt you have Fox blood in your veins."

"So, what is it you want me to do, exactly?"

"You remember I talked about the Yianni brothers?"

I recalled the name coming up in conversation over the Foxes' dinner table, but it rang as few bells with me now as it had then. "I think so."

"But you've never had any dealings with them?"

I shook my head. Before Cameron could say any more, Millie arrived at our table carrying a tray.

"Here's your tea, Cameron. Strong, just a tiny bit of milk." She set a mug in front of him.

Cameron took a sip of his tea, and a smile creased his face. "Oh, this is perfect. The next time I bring Mum on one of her shopping trips, we're stopping off here for refreshments." Once Millie had accepted his praise with a faint colouring of her cheeks and gone off to clear away plates from a recently vacated table, Cameron returned to what we'd been discussing before the interruption. "Costas and Lazaros Yianni are old acquaintances of ours. They're two of the best counterfeiters in the country. You get one of their forged twenty-quid notes, you'll never tell it apart from the real thing. They run a handful of businesses — a Greek restaurant on Green Lanes, a couple of barber's shops, a shawarma house not far from the Emirates Stadium — that they use to distribute their forgeries. The customer comes in for a haircut, they're slipped a dodgy tenner in their change, and before you know it, that money is in circulation somewhere on the other side of London."

"And how does this affect me, exactly?"

"Costas owed my dad a lot of dosh, his share of a deal they did a while back. You don't need to know the details, but we're talking a high six-figure sum here. All that matters is he hadn't paid up when Dad died. Connor spoke to him, and he promises we'll get what he owes, but he keeps stalling, and we think he's planning to settle his debt with counterfeit currency. And fifty quid, a hundred quid, I could spend that without thinking about it, but there's no way we'll be able to dispose of several hundred thousand pounds of funny money without someone cottoning on. So, we're planning to get what we're due another way."

"Go on…" I found myself leaning closer to Cameron across the table, curious as to what he had in mind.

"The Yianni family have another business — a jeweller's shop just off Chapel Market. They sell a lot of status symbol watches. You know, the kind that cost more than most people earn in a year. So, our intention is to rob the shop. We reckon an armful of Rolexes should cover everything we're owed, and if the Yiannis are properly insured, they'll be able to put in a claim for whatever we take. In theory, they won't lose out, but we'll have made our point, and maybe that mug Costas will respect our family a little more in future."

I couldn't help but admire the thought the brothers had put into their plan. "Clever. But I still don't see why you need me as part of all this."

"Well, at first, we thought we'd break in after the shop closes for the night. But that's a lot of hard work when there's a much simpler way of doing it. All we need to do is have one person go into the shop, make out they're looking to buy a watch, ask to see some of the most expensive ones. Then the rest of us steam in, threaten the assistant and grab as many watches as we can. But the problem with that is, it's most likely going to be one of the Yiannis working behind the counter — their dad, or their sister Athena. And they know me, Connor and Callum, and they'd be able to describe us to the police. But you… They don't have a clue who you are. All you'd have to do is pretend to be an ordinary customer—"

"And if I refuse?" Already all the ways in which this situation might go wrong flashed before my eyes.

Now it was Cameron's turn to lean in, and his expression was less than friendly. "We've done our homework on you, Kyle. We know how you earn your living, who supplies you, the kind of places you sell that poisonous stuff. All it would take would be one anonymous phone call to the police and *boof!*" He snapped his fingers. "Another dealer taken off the streets."

Nausea churned in my gut. Until this moment, I figured I'd listen politely to Cameron's plan, then tell him thanks but no thanks. But he held all the cards, and he knew it. He sat back, waiting for my reply.

"Okay, I'll do it. I'll help you rob the Yiannis."

I sank back in my seat. My gaze locked with Millie's as she stood by the table next to ours. I wasn't sure how much of our conversation she'd overheard as she stacked the dirty crockery onto a tray, but from the dismay in her expression, I knew it had been more than enough to destroy her trust in me all over again.

Chapter Twenty-One

Millie

"So, you're going to take part in a robbery." I fought to keep my voice low. I'd waited till Cameron Fox had finished his tea, given Kyle a big, back-slapping hug, dropped a handful of pound coins on the table and sauntered out of the café. Then I'd left Jasmine in charge of the counter and taken Kyle through to the cramped stock room at the back of the building so we could talk. It was the one place I knew no one would be able to eavesdrop on us. I was sick to my stomach over what I'd caught Kyle discussing with Cameron Fox — even more so when I'd watched them laughing and bidding fond farewells to each other — and the sooner we thrashed this out the better.

"What exactly did you hear?" It wasn't a denial, and Kyle fixed me with a hard stare, as if he'd expected me to call him out on his plotting.

"Almost nothing. Only the name...Yianni?" I pushed my hands into my hair, wanting to ease the tension headache building at my temples. "Don't worry, Kyle, I don't have a clue who that is, if you're worried that I might be thinking of giving them a heads-up."

"Millie, listen—" Kyle grabbed hold of my arm and pulled me closer to him. His expression softened as he tried to turn his charm on me, but it wasn't working for him right now. My anger couldn't be mollified by the twinkle in his blue eyes and the way his cheeks dimpled as he smiled. Not when he'd taken my trust in him that he'd worked so hard to restore and smashed it to pieces.

"No, you listen to me. When we got back together, it was on the understanding that you would keep whatever dodgy activity you're involved with well away from me. No dealing anywhere near the shop, no trying to launder your dirty money through my till, nothing that would bring the police to my door. So, what happens? You invite Cameron bloody Fox here for a cuppa and a cosy chat about this heist you're working on together."

"Hey, hey. First off, I did not invite Cameron here. He just turned up out of the blue, okay? But now he needs my help, and I wasn't going to tell him no."

"Oh, really? Are you totally stupid?" I snapped, shrugging out of Kyle's grasp. "You know the kind of luck that follows him around. His father was shot dead, his sister-in-law almost died in a car crash… That family seems to have a habit of pissing the wrong people off, and you're happy to be a part of it?"

For the first time, Kyle's gaze clouded. "I didn't have a choice."

I threw my hands up in the air, unable to believe what I was hearing. "Of course you did. You could have chosen to tell him you don't want to be any part of his dangerous little caper." I went to leave the room, needing to get away from Kyle before I really lost my temper, but he pulled me back and spun me around to face him.

"No, I couldn't. Listen to me for one moment. Cameron made it very clear that if I don't help him rob the Yiannis, then he will shop me to the police as a drug dealer. And the things I've done, if my case went to trial, I could be looking at ten years in prison easily — less if I plead guilty, but still..."

"He'd do that to — ?" I almost said, 'his own brother', but I wasn't convinced that was how any of the Foxes regarded Kyle, except maybe Lynda. "That's a hell of a hold to have over you."

"You think I don't know that?" Kyle gave a bitter, hollow laugh. "Cameron's got my balls in a vice, and he's revelling in it. The only good part of this is that it's strictly a one-time deal. I help them with this robbery and" — he cast his eyes to the floor, not wanting to meet my gaze — "I become a full-fledged member of the Fox family."

"So, that's what this is really about."

I should have known. It's always family first with the Foxes. Blood overrides every other consideration — and Kyle isn't any different, even though I dared to hope he might be.

"You know how much this means to me." Kyle's voice was strained, and he had the haunted look of an animal that had been caught in a trap. "The only thing that means more is you. You've got to believe me, Millie."

"I'd like to, honestly, I would, but you make it so difficult for me. I'm starting to think maybe our getting back together was a huge mistake."

"And if we hadn't, would you be standing here now, in this beautiful little café with a queue of customers out of the door almost every morning and a mention in a *Time Out* article on the best places to grab coffee and a cake in North London?"

Whatever sharp retort I'd been about to give him died on my lips. I couldn't deny Kyle's backing had helped me secure the lease to the Bellariva. Without his help, I'd most likely still be trying to scrape together enough money to meet the rental premium on some rundown place that was twice as far out of Central London as this one. I might have thoughts right now of telling him I could manage on my own, but deep down, I was all too aware how much I needed him. I'd tried to walk away from him once and found it impossible to do. His hold on my heart was too strong. I would never truly be free of him, and I knew I didn't want to be.

What I eventually said was, "So, you take part in this one robbery and that's all you have to do for him."

"Cameron Fox may be a lot of things, but if he promises you something, he won't go back on it. And I am determined that I am going to keep you completely in the dark about all this. You clearly don't know who the Yiannis are, and I'm going to make sure it stays like that. So long as you have no idea where and when any of this is going to take place, there's no way you can be viewed as an accessory."

When he mentioned that, it gave me reason to pause. I didn't know much about how the criminal justice system worked — I'd never as much as been called on to do jury duty — but I'd seen enough crime dramas on TV to know that even being tangentially involved with a crime could be enough to land you in a lot of trouble.

"So, I'm just going to spend the next few weeks on tenterhooks, wondering if every day is the day I suddenly have to find myself providing an alibi for you?"

"Millie, you know what I do for a living. Has it never crossed your mind you might have to do that for me already?"

I sagged back against a box containing paper cake cases, the elegant rose-pink ones I'd been using since the first day I'd started offering cupcakes for sale. Something at the back of my mind reminded me the box was almost empty, meaning I'd need to order more soon, but the mundane details of running my business were the last thing on my mind right now.

Sometimes, it was easy to forget Kyle was a criminal, that every time he answered a phone call or went to run an errand, he could be supplying someone with a few grams of cocaine. Someone who might easily turn out to be an undercover policeman looking to make an arrest. But right now, in this claustrophobic room filled with all manner of catering supplies, the uncomfortable truth of our life together was impossible to ignore.

"I really don't want you to do this," I muttered.

"I know, and I wish I had some other choice, but I don't." Kyle reached for the door handle, unable to meet my gaze. "Just try to forget I ever told you anything about what Cameron's planning. It'll be easier if you do."

He slipped out of the room like a guilty man, leaving me to wonder quite what trouble he was stirring up by agreeing to this dangerous proposal. Nothing between us would ever be easy — at least, not until Cameron and the rest of the Foxes gave Kyle the place in their family that he so desperately craved.

Chapter Twenty-Two

Millie

I trudged up Pentonville Road in the swirling rain, headphones jammed in my ears and the soothing strains of a Chopin piano sonata doing nothing to lift my mood. Last night on the way back home, the chain on my bike had snapped. I needed to schedule a repair, but this morning I'd had too many other tasks to even think about finding someone to do the necessary work.

First, I'd had to mail out the online orders for letterbox brownies that had come in over the past few days. I hated the main post office at Mount Pleasant — there never seemed to be enough counter staff working, and the queue ahead of me moved with all the speed of an arthritic snail — but it was the nearest branch to home.

Once I'd finally had each of my stack of parcels weighed in turn and the appropriate postage applied, I was free to make my way to the next spot on my list of errands. I needed blackberries and pears for the muffins I planned to make, and Chapel Market was the best place to buy them in quantity, even if I couldn't carry as much by hand as I would have been able to transport in the pod of my bike.

I turned left down a side street, to cut off the busy corner where Pentonville Road met Islington High Street. A white van sped by, driving straight through a puddle and splashing me from head to foot with cold, dirty water. My mood soured even further, and I hurried on, head down against the eddies of wind whipped up in the van's wake. I consoled myself with the thought that once I got to the café, I could make myself a coffee and take a few moments to warm up before I got down to the serious business of baking.

Ahead of me, the market was in full swing, with stalls selling everything from fruit and vegetables to sets of saucepans and cheap copies of designer handbags. Stallholders shouted their wares, and music blared out from half a dozen radios, all tuned to different channels. The place had an air of controlled chaos, and the noise and bustle helped to lighten the gloom that had settled over me.

As if to prove my day was getting better, I spotted a familiar figure standing up ahead. Even in a nondescript dark waterproof jacket with the hood pulled up, Kyle was immediately recognisable. Forgetting about my shopping list and the chores waiting for me in the café, I dashed over and flung my arms around him.

"Hey, stranger, fancy bumping into you."

He gazed at me, startled, and took a step back to release himself from my embrace. "Millie...what are you doing here?"

I'd never known him not be pleased to see me, but the rigid set of his body language made me feel as if he didn't want me anywhere near him. He glanced around, as if he were keeping an eye out for someone approaching.

Oh, shit. Is he waiting here to sell drugs to someone?

Even as the thought went through my mind, Kyle seemed to recover himself. "Sorry, you surprised me. Shouldn't you be at the café?"

"I had errands to run. Seems like fate wanted our paths to cross today."

"I don't know that I'd call it fate," he said, half to himself. Then he brightened, as if he'd come to some kind of decision. "Actually, now you're here, there is something you can help me out with." Before I knew what was happening, Kyle was steering me along the pavement and through the door of a small jeweller's shop.

A neatly dressed dark-haired girl in her early twenties greeted us with a cosmetically whitened smile as we walked in. "Good morning. How can I help you both today?" With no other customers in the shop, her focus was completely on us.

As we approached the counter, a display of rings in the glass-fronted cabinet beneath it caught my eye. Beautifully cut diamonds, sapphires, rubies and precious stones I couldn't put a name to glimmered in the light, and I realised why Kyle had looked so flustered when I'd run into him outside. He must have come here to choose an engagement ring, hoping he could do it at a time when I was busy in the café, and I'd caught him out.

What are you going to say if he asks you to marry him?

Even as I considered it, I knew my answer would have to be no. As much as I loved Kyle, my trust in him was still fragile, and his willingness to get involved with the Foxes in a robbery made me question how much he cared about me in return.

Luckily, Kyle spared me from my dilemma. "We're here to look at watches," he told her. "You have a couple in the window I was interested in."

"Of course, sir. And which would those be?"

"You have a Rolex with a red ombre dial, and another that's silver with a honeycomb dial. And there's a Patek Philippe with an olive-green strap I'm drawn to as well, but I'd like to see how they look on my wrist."

The assistant bobbed her head. "You have a good eye, sir. I'll just go and fetch those for you to try. Though the last one you mentioned is pre-owned. I trust that's not a problem?"

"Not at all. I'm sure whoever wore it before would be happy to know it'll be going to a good home."

As women usually did, the assistant melted under the full-force attack of Kyle's twinkly charm, and she hurried to retrieve the items he'd described.

I shifted from foot to foot and wondered how long it would take Kyle to make his choice, conscious that I still had fruit to buy and muffins to bake.

"Here you are, sir." The assistant brought out a small black velvet cushion with the watches laid out on it. "I hope you don't mind, but I also chose another two that might be the kind of thing you're looking for."

"That's very thoughtful of you" — Kyle squinted at the discreet metal name badge fastened to the assistant's blouse — "Athena." He picked up the silver Rolex and slipped it around his wrist. "What do you think, Millie?" he asked, holding up his arm so we could both admire the way it looked.

"Honestly? I'm not quite sure it's you." Among everything Athena had brought out, my eye was drawn to the watch with the green strap. "Why not try that one instead?" I suggested, pointing to it. "It's not at all flashy, and it will suit your colouring better."

"Yeah, you might be right." Kyle took off the Rolex and replaced it with the one I'd chosen. He was admiring it in the mirror that stood on the counter, twisting his wrist this way and that, when his phone buzzed. He brought it out of his pocket and glanced at it. I assumed he'd received some kind of notification, but whatever it was couldn't have been important, as he simply tapped the screen, then put the phone away.

A moment later, the door to the shop burst open and two men ran in. They were both dressed from head to foot in black and wore balaclavas to conceal their features. I couldn't be sure, but one of them appeared to be holding a gun. I only had the briefest of glimpses of it before Kyle put an arm around me and gathered me to him.

"Kyle, what's happening?" I whispered, even though it was all too clear these men were intent on robbing the place.

They didn't go for the till. Instead, they started scooping up the watches Athena had brought out for Kyle and stuffing them into a small black backpack.

"We have to get out of here, please," I begged Kyle, afraid that once they'd taken whatever they wanted from the shop, they might turn their attention to us.

"Don't worry," Kyle murmured into my hair. "It's going to be all right, I promise."

Even as he spoke, an alarm blared out, high-pitched and deafening. I assumed Athena must have pressed a hidden button beneath the counter. Despite the noise, the two robbers didn't pause in what they were doing. The one with the gun used the butt of it to smash the front of a display cabinet and helped himself to a handful of gold chains. His companion grabbed his hand and tried to get him to stop, appearing to mouth the words, "We got what we came for," but he carried on dropping them into the backpack with single-minded purpose.

Athena made a dash for the door behind her. She wrenched it open and began yelling in a language I didn't understand. Given her name, I thought it might be Greek. Her speech was fast and frantic, the terror obvious in her voice, but I caught what might have been the name 'Costas'. Seconds later, a thickset man with curly dark hair and a thick growth of stubble on his chin emerged from the back of the shop. His bulk filled the doorway, and he radiated menace. Like one of the thieves, he also carried a gun and his finger rested on the trigger.

A shot rang out. It hit the man who'd been stealing necklaces square in the shoulder. He screamed and collapsed to the floor. The other robber got to his knees beside him and checked the extent of the damage to his arm, then looked up at us.

"For God's sake, you've got to help him or he's going to bleed out." He sounded genuinely anguished. "Millie, come here and put pressure on the wound." For a moment, my knees threatened to give way. How did this stranger know my name?

He's no stranger. Don't pretend you don't know that voice.

He turned his gaze on me, and I saw for the first time familiar blue eyes of Cameron Fox. I was sure if I looked at the injured robber, he'd be a Fox, too. As the pieces fell into place, I sagged in Kyle's arms. How had I not realised what was really happening the second the robbers stormed into the shop? The notification on his phone must have been some signal between the brothers and Kyle, letting him know they were on their way. He'd wanted to keep me as far away as he could from the heist the family had cooked up between them, deliberately keeping me ignorant of their intended target, yet I'd managed to stumble right into the middle of it.

"She moves an inch, and I shoot her too. That goes for the rest of you." The man I believed to be called Costas levelled the barrel of the gun at us. I'd never seen a sawn-off shotgun anywhere than in a TV crime drama, but I was staring at one now. I'd already learned how much damage it could do from the spreading pool of blood on the floorboards and the pained whimpers of Cameron's brother, and Costas seemed perfectly prepared to act on his threat.

"Cameron, it hurts so much…"

Cameron blanched at the sound of his brother's voice. We couldn't let him die, no matter what Costas said. Instinctively, I broke free of Kyle's embrace so I could get to him and try to stem the bleeding as Cameron had asked.

"I said stay where you are, bitch." From behind me, I heard a click. Costas must have cocked the trigger again. When I swivelled my head to look at him, the gun was aimed straight at my chest. His expression was cold, emotionless, and I knew my life meant nothing to him. I closed my eyes and thought of all the things that Kyle and I would never do together, and all the many times I should have told him how much I loved him.

This is it. I'm going to die…

"Sod that." Kyle spoke in the tone of a man who wouldn't stand for my being threatened. "Cam, you got what you came for and now we need to go before the police get here. This fucker won't try anything." He gestured to Costas. "He thinks he's the big man but he's all talk."

The bullet whistling inches past me proved Kyle wrong. It slammed into a tall, free-standing cabinet that exploded in a shower of glass fragments. Cameron grabbed me and pulled me down to the floor so I wouldn't get hit by one of the dozens of shards flying through the air.

There was a second shot. Athena shrieked. When I risked raising my head enough to peek in her direction, I saw Costas staggering backward, blood staining the front of his white shirt. I glanced over to Kyle and saw him holding the gun, the look on his face suggesting he couldn't believe he'd fired it.

Beneath the wailing of the shop's alarms and Athena's panicked cries of, "No, no, Costas, please be okay...", I swore I heard a police siren — faint for now but steadily coming closer. Kyle was right, we had to leave.

Cameron recovered his composure the fastest of the three of us. "Millie, Kyle, help me with Connor," he said. Between us, we managed to raise the barely conscious Connor to his feet. Kyle took most of his weight, mindful of the shattered bones in his shoulder, and together he and I guided him out of the shop.

Curious heads turned our way as we stumbled away from the jeweller's shop. I supposed it wasn't every day a man wearing a balaclava and bleeding heavily emerged into the miserable winter weather, supported by two people whose faces were frozen with shock.

We made our way down the road to the place where Cameron and Connor had parked their getaway car. Cameron ran on ahead to start the engine. When Kyle and I caught up to him, he dragged Connor in through the back passenger door with less care for his injuries than I might have expected, then tossed the backpack full of watches and jewellery onto the floor at his feet.

"Okay, Millie, you get in with Connor," Cameron ordered. "There should be a travel rug in the back. Wad it up, press it to the wound as hard as you can and just keep it in place till we get to the hospital."

"Hospital?" Kyle echoed, taking the front seat beside Cameron. "Where are we taking him?"

"University College," Cameron replied as he put the car into gear and pulled away from the kerb with a squeal of brakes. "And just to warn you, I'm not in the mood to stop for any red lights."

Chapter Twenty-Three

Kyle

"How's he holding up?" Cameron addressed Millie in the back seat, but he kept his eyes fixed on the road ahead. They were the first words he'd spoken since we'd left Chapel Market, and fear and tension hung heavy between all of us in the car.

"I think I've managed to stem the bleeding for now, but he's drifting in and out of consciousness." She didn't look up, instead focusing all her energy on the task of tending to Connor, who lay sprawled across the faux leather seat, moaning in pain. A spot of blood had soaked through the tartan travel rug Millie had pressed to his injured shoulder. "Come on, Connor, don't go to sleep. Stay with me," she urged him.

Ahead of us, the traffic began to slow as it approached the turn-off for St Pancras station. Cameron spun the wheel and swerved around a bus that had stopped to pick up passengers. He almost collided with a van coming in the opposite direction.

"Jesus, Cam," I muttered as the van driver pounded on his horn and gave us the middle finger through his windscreen. "Millie's trying to save Connor's life and you're doing your best to get him killed." Cameron turned his head and glared at me, and I raised my hands in apology. "Look, all I'm saying is maybe you don't need to take so many risks. We're nearly at the hospital. You can afford to slow down a little."

As if in direct defiance of my suggestion, Cameron stamped on the accelerator and weaved his way across a crowded box junction as the lights turned from amber to red. "I just don't want my brother to die." His voice was tight, strained. Until now, I'd never seen him look in the least vulnerable. I could tell how much he was struggling not to give in to his fear of losing Connor the same way he'd so recently lost his father.

"He's not going to die," I assured him, even though I couldn't speak with any certainty.

"Why did I never stop to think Costas Yianni might be in the shop today?" Cameron said, half to himself. I knew he must be replaying in his head every moment since he'd entered the jeweller's, just as I was.

"You couldn't have known it was going to happen. From what you told me the guy oversees half a dozen businesses scattered across North London. Him being there was simply bad luck on our part."

"Yeah, and it ended up with Connor taking a bullet..." Cameron shook his head, managing to recover himself. "But you —" He risked a glance at me and his face cracked into an admiring smile. "Where did you learn to handle a gun like that?"

"I didn't. I've never even seen one up close before today," I admitted. "But as soon as it seemed like Costas was going to hurt Millie, I knew I had to stop him." I looked out of the passenger-side window, reliving the instant when I'd snatched the gun up from where it lay close to Connor's side. The weight of it in my hand. The surprising ease with which I'd pulled the trigger. The recoil of the weapon and the acrid smell of smoke in the air. Bright-red blood on Costas' shirt. "I just hope I didn't kill him. I don't think I could live with myself if…"

"Don't." Cameron moved his hand from the steering wheel and squeezed my forearm. "You did what you had to. If it was Em he was going to shoot, I would have done exactly the same."

Up ahead, I saw the round Underground sign jutting out from the front of Euston Square Tube station. The impressive modern University College Hospital building, with its distinctive green glass windows, occupied the next block, and Cameron indicated to turn left so we could park up. The clock on the dashboard touchscreen showed that less than ten minutes had passed since we'd made our escape from the Yiannis' shop, and still I worried that we hadn't arrived in time to save Connor's life.

"It's okay, Connor. We'll be there in a minute," Millie said, as Connor groaned and clutched at her arm with his good hand. She glanced over at me. Though she radiated calm whenever she dealt with Connor, the freckles stood out on her stricken face and her eyes shone with unshed tears. I realised how deeply she'd been affected by what she'd witnessed during the robbery, and I wanted to put my arms around her and never let go.

A thought occurred to me. "What are we going to say when the hospital staff ask what happened to Connor?"

Cameron shrugged. "We tell them he got shot."

"But—" Thoughts raced through my mind of all the questions that would inevitably raise.

"They're not going to ask why, or who did it. They just need the basic information, so they know what kind of injuries they're dealing with. They'll leave everything else in the hands of the police." Cameron spoke with a matter-of-fact tone, and I reckoned he must have been remembering what had happened with Charlie. Though from what I recalled of the press coverage of that incident, Charlie Fox had been dead on arrival at the hospital, whereas Connor was weak but very much still alive. "Anyway, we're here now. Let's just get Connor into A&E and they can take care of him." He shut off the engine, but before he got out of the car, he turned to Millie. "I'm sorry you had to get caught up in this. When I saw you in the jeweller's, I didn't know what the hell Kyle was playing at, bringing you in there, after all he'd said about needing to keep you well away from what we'd planned."

"I didn't intend to," I said. "But we bumped into each other on the street and...well, I had to improvise."

"It was a stroke of genius, mind." It was the last thing I'd expected to hear Cameron say. "I mean, who's going to be suspicious of a couple going in to look at watches? But don't worry, we're never going to ask you to do anything like that again." He unbuckled his seatbelt and got out of the car. I followed, and we went round to the rear door to help Connor.

Before Cameron opened the door, he pulled me into an embrace. He clapped a hand to my shoulder and put his mouth close to my ear. "What you did today, you've proved you deserve your place in our family...brother."

Hearing that word from Cameron's lips had me buzzing, like it filled a gap in my soul I hadn't known existed. But this moment wasn't about me and how I fitted with the rest of the Foxes. It was about making sure Connor got the medical attention he needed.

As soon as Cameron and I strode through the front doors of the accident and emergency unit, supporting Connor between us, we were approached by two members of the medical staff. They took him from us and hurried away. Cameron followed them, answering questions that were being fired at him by a nurse in dark-blue scrubs.

Millie wobbled on her feet, and I took her in my arms, afraid she was about to faint. I wasn't too happy in this frenetic, antiseptic-smelling environment myself. It reminded me too much of the fact that Mum was lying in her bed in the hospice, hooked up to the machines monitoring her vital signs.

"Come on, let's get you home."

She shook her head. "I need to go to the café. I've got so much to do. I never even got the blackberries I—"

I cut her off. "I'll ring them and tell them you're not coming in. If Jasmine asks, I'll say you've picked up some sickness bug that's going round. I'm sure she can cope without you for the rest of the day."

"I suppose you're right." She didn't sound entirely convinced, but I knew how hard Millie found it to leave someone else in charge of her business, even for a few hours.

She appeared to have gone through hell, her hair coming loose from its braid and her clothes soaked with Connor's blood. I guessed I didn't look any better myself. "Somehow, I don't think they'll let us in a taxi like this. And I don't fancy getting on the Tube with everyone staring at us. Will you be okay to walk?"

"Yeah." She gave me a smile. It was only a weak one but still it reassured me that today's events hadn't completely broken her. "I think the fresh air will do me good."

I wrapped an arm around her shoulders and led her out to the street.

Chapter Twenty-Four

Millie

For once, Kyle was waiting for me in the lobby when I arrived at the block of flats. I'd grown used to him buzzing me up to his floor, but today he stood with a smile on his face and what appeared to be a black scarf in his hands.

"Before we go upstairs…" As he spoke, he wrapped the scarf around my eyes and tied it in place, forming a makeshift blindfold.

"Kyle, what are you doing?" I thought back to all the kinky games we'd played together and wondered whether this was the start of a new one. The idea of submitting to him always appealed to me, but I wasn't sure how I felt about doing it in such a public place.

"I have a surprise for you, and I don't want you to see it until everything's ready."

A bell pinged before I could ask any more questions, and I realised the lift had arrived. Kyle put his arms around my shoulders and guided me through the doors. I really hoped there was no one around to see us. I hadn't heard footsteps or voices, but that didn't mean someone else wasn't in here with us. I didn't know whether that alarmed me or added a new level of excitement to whatever Kyle had in mind for me.

My mind raced as the lift came to a halt and Kyle steered me out and down the hallway to his flat. Even once we were inside, he didn't remove the scarf. I stood, trying to make out any clues as to what he had planned for me. When I strained my ears, I thought I picked up the faint splash of running water, but I couldn't be sure.

"So now are you going to tell me what's going on?" I asked, impatient to be free of the blindfold.

Kyle's feet shuffled somewhere close by me. "Well, after everything we've been through, I really wanted to take you away to a fancy spa for a couple of days, but I can't risk leaving London right now, not with Mum…"

He didn't need to say anything else. Yesterday, he'd taken me to the hospice so I could finally meet his mother for the first time. It had been a briefer visit than Kyle had intended, as she could barely keep her eyes open due to the high level of pain relief she'd been given. When she'd taken hold of my hand and told me to look after her boy when she was gone, I'd promised I would in a voice I hadn't been able to prevent from shaking.

"It's okay," I assured him.

"So, I thought what I should do instead is bring the spa to you." Kyle grasped my shoulders and turned me to the left. We walked a few paces, then a door clicked open, and he ushered me through it.

He unknotted the scarf and pulled it from my eyes with a deft flourish. We were in his bathroom. I hadn't been mistaken about the sound of water. The taps were on, and the tub was almost full to the brim. As Kyle turned them off, I took a moment to admire what he'd done to give the room a spa-like atmosphere. He'd acquired a couple of small potted ferns and put them on the shelves, and several thick white pillar candles flickered, casting a soft glow over the tiles. A stack of fluffy white towels had been placed by the bathtub, and the air was perfumed with lavender.

"And for the final touch..." Kyle reached over to a small teal and white device attached to the inside of the bath. He flicked a switch on the front of it and immediately jets of water began streaming out, frothing up the surface and recreating the feel of a hot tub.

"Clever, huh? The things they sell online these days." He sounded pleased with himself, and I couldn't blame him. He'd clearly spent a lot of time putting this together for my benefit, and I dropped a gentle kiss on his cheek.

"Thanks for doing this."

"For you, anything." He tapped at his phone, and music began to play. The simple piano melody, set against a background of echoing harmonies, sounded exactly like something you'd hear while you were receiving a treatment in an upmarket spa. "Now, get undressed and climb in. I'll be back in a moment with the cocktails."

Today was getting more decadent by the moment, but I couldn't think of a nicer way to spend a lazy Sunday. I slipped out of my clothes and arranged them in a neat pile on the wooden bathroom stool. By the time Kyle returned, a champagne flute in each hand, I wore only my lacy blue boy shorts. I went to remove them, but he shook his head.

"Let me do that." He set our drinks down next to the pile of towels and came close so he could peel my underwear down. The gesture was intimate, Kyle's breath warm on the side of my neck as he undressed me, and I shivered.

Once I was naked, I climbed into the bath. I settled back, enjoying how the water churned around me. Kyle handed me my glass, and I sipped from it. "This is nice. What is it?"

"A champagne cocktail." Kyle stripped off his T-shirt. "I didn't want to make anything that involves all that Tom Cruise-style tossing the cocktail shaker in the air, and these were so simple. Champagne, brandy, some bitters splashed onto a sugar cube…"

I set my glass on the lip of the tub and rested my head back so I could watch as Kyle removed the rest of his clothing. When he peeled down his boxer-briefs, his cock was already half hard and I put out a hand to brush my fingertips over its plump head as he got into the bath.

"Don't tease me," he murmured. "There'll be time for that later."

We arranged ourselves so that he was behind me, cradling me with a leg on either side of my body. I relaxed against his warm, solid chest and reached for my drink again.

"So, the good news is I got a call from Cameron," Kyle said, "and he told me he went to see Connor in the hospital."

"That's good news?" I wasn't sure I wanted to talk about this right now, not when I was so comfortable in Kyle's arms and the rest of the world seemed a million miles away.

"Yeah, he said the doctors are so pleased with how Connor's recovering from the surgery on his shoulder, they're planning to release him in the next couple of days. They have warned that he may never get the full range of motion back in that arm, but it sounds like it could have been so much worse. If we hadn't got him there as soon as we did after he was shot, there's a strong possibility they would have had to amputate it."

When I glanced over to the vanity unit, I caught a glimpse of Kyle's Patek Phillipe watch with its distinctive olive-green strap. He'd still been wearing it when we'd carried Connor out of the Yiannis' shop, and when he'd tried to give it to Cameron as part of the spoils of the robbery, Cameron had told him after everything he'd done, he'd earned the right to keep it.

I bit my lip as unwelcome memories of that morning flooded back. I didn't want to ask, recalling the moment when I'd stared down the stubby barrel of that shotgun, but I had to. "What about Costas Yianni? Is he —? I mean, he didn't die, did he?"

"No, Cameron has been asking around and by all accounts he's fine. When I shot him, I only grazed his side. He got a couple of cracked ribs, but nothing worse than that. Though I wouldn't be shedding a tear for him if he had died, even if it meant I'd be looking at serious jail time. Not after he tried to kill you."

"You really think there's a possibility you'll go to prison for this?" Part of me was surprised detectives hadn't come looking for Kyle and the Fox brothers already.

"Apparently, the local plod has been asking questions. There might be witnesses who saw us leaving the shop, but I have no idea if anyone got a good look at us, and Costas is refusing to press any charges. He won't say anything about who robbed him, or who shot him. Cameron reckons he's worried that if he points the finger at the Foxes, they'll just turn around and tell the police everything they know about all his dodgy dealings. And if they do, there's no way he's not going down for a long time, too." He took a long drink. When he set his glass down again, it was empty. "It doesn't mean they won't come after us for this, but there's no CCTV in that shop, which makes their job harder, and if they think it's just a couple of local lowlifes trying to take each other out, they may decide it's more trouble than it's worth to investigate."

I didn't say anything. I hated to think the shadow of all this would keep hanging over us, but Kyle seemed optimistic that he and the brothers would get away with it. I thought of what Kyle had told me about the other gang leader who'd ended up dead when he'd crossed the Foxes. It seemed like Cameron really did lead a charmed life, and I had no idea how long that kind of luck could continue.

"Anyway," Kyle went on, "I don't want to think about any of this now. Let's just clear our minds of everything and relax…"

He carded his fingers through my hair as I closed my eyes and listened to the simple, soothing music. Part of me thought I could lie there all day, breathing in the scent of lavender and sipping my delicious cocktail, but it couldn't have been more than a few minutes before Kyle stirred behind me.

"I don't know about you, but I'm ready to take this to the bedroom."

Chapter Twenty-Five

Millie

Kyle's erect cock pressed at the small of my back, clear evidence of his excitement. He helped me to stand and get out of the bath. When he wrapped a towel around me, I sank into his embrace. I couldn't remember the last time I'd been so thoroughly pampered, and I loved this thoughtful, caring side of him.

I pushed aside the cynical thought that this show of devotion might be fuelled by his guilt at getting me mixed up in the robbery at the jeweller's and allowed him to lead me through to his bedroom.

"Lie down on the bed," he said. "I have a present for you."

"Thank you, but you really shouldn't have." He'd spoiled me enough already with his homemade hot tub. He didn't need to give me gifts, too.

"Honestly, it's nothing much. Just some body lotion to finish off your spa treatment." He reached into the drawer of his nightstand and brought out a paper carrier bag bearing the Jo Malone logo.

"Oh, you shouldn't have," I told him, knowing whatever he'd bought wouldn't have come cheaply.

"Hey, if I can't treat the woman I love every now and again…" He sat on the bed and patted the space beside him. "Come on, make yourself comfortable."

I rolled onto my front as he unscrewed the lid of the tub. He pulled the towel out from underneath me and massaged a little of the rich lotion into my skin. I sighed as the heady scent of myrrh hit my nostrils. Any lingering tension in my shoulders melted away as Kyle worked his hands over my back in broad, sweeping circles.

"Have you ever thought about becoming a professional masseur?" I asked. "You're really good at this."

"Maybe I just know where you like to be touched."

I couldn't fail to pick up on the innuendo in his words, and I shivered with thoughts of what might be to come once he finished his massage.

He smoothed lotion along my arms and legs, then closed the tub. Out of the corner of my eye, I saw him fishing in the nightstand drawer again. This time, he produced a bottle of lube and I knew things were about to get a lot more intimate.

"Close your eyes for me, Millie."

I did as he requested and lay still. He put his lips to the nape of my neck and kissed a soft trail down my back. My nipples grew hard, pressing against the covers beneath me, as he took his time exploring my body with his mouth. Acting on instinct, I spread my legs, hoping he might kiss me there, too, but when he reached the small of my back and pulled away from me, I realised he had other plans in mind.

I didn't see him open the lube, but I heard the pop of the cap, followed by the sounds of him squeezing what sounded like a good amount out of the bottle. When I turned my head in the hope that he might let me watch him, his response was immediate. "Just keep your eyes closed," he ordered me. I didn't know what he intended to do next, but that was all part of the fun.

He traced his hand, slick with lube, down the cleft between my cheeks. When he slid a finger in my pussy, followed swiftly by a second pressing into my rear hole, I bit back a sob. It felt so deliciously naughty to be filled front and back, and I wanted more.

"Do you like that?" he said, his mouth close to my ear as he moved those fingers slowly to-and-fro inside me.

"You know I do."

"Do you want me to slide my cock in there?"

I knew exactly what he meant by 'there', and I hesitated, torn between apprehension and excitement. "I..."

He must have picked up on my doubt, because he stopped thrusting his fingers into me. "Hey, if you're not ready, that's okay. We can try some other time. This is all about giving you pleasure, don't forget."

I nodded. "I know, and right now, I just want you to fuck me."

"Now, that I can do."

He lifted himself off me, and a moment later I heard the tell-tale noise of a condom packet being torn open. I turned over to enjoy the sight of Kyle giving his cock a few slow jerks with his fist before he slid the rubber down over it. I didn't think I'd ever grow tired of watching him pleasure himself.

Without another word, he spread my legs wide apart and got into position between them. Never breaking eye contact, he eased his whole length into me with one gentle push. He held still for a few seconds, and I clenched my pussy muscles around his shaft.

"Oh, yeah. You're so tight," Kyle groaned. "It's like you were made for me."

"We were made for each other," I told him. "I only wish it hadn't taken me so long to figure it out."

My words seemed to spur him into action, and he began to fuck me with gentle rocking motions of his hips. Little eddies of pleasure stirred in me, and I sighed as he reached between my legs and teased my clit. I didn't need to tell him where to touch me. My soft murmurs and the way I pushed my hands through his hair must have let him know the effect he was having on me.

Slowly but surely, he speeded up the pace. I arched my body up with each one, matching him stroke for stroke. Driven wild with passion, I dug my fingers into his sweat-dampened shoulders, urging him to go harder, faster. The bedframe banged against the wall, and the scent of our lovemaking mingled with the heady mix of myrrh and vanilla that coated my skin.

With one last thrust, Kyle brought me to my peak. The rippling of my pussy around his shaft triggered his orgasm, and he called out my name, lost in his own pleasure.

As he started to soften, he slipped out of me and rolled onto his back, pulling me onto his chest as he did. When he spoke again, his voice was deep and throaty.

"You know, I'm starting to realise how lucky I am to have you. I thought being a Fox was what I really wanted, but now they've accepted me into the family, I realise that without you it wouldn't mean anything. You make me a better man, Millie, and I love you so much."

I reacted to his heartfelt declaration by resting my head on his chest so I could be soothed by the strong, steady beat of his heart. "And I love you, too."

"When I think how close I came to losing you…" He shifted on the bed, pulling me more tightly to him. "From now on, I am going to make sure nothing like that ever happens again."

Lying cradled in his arms, I knew he meant it. As his breathing grew more even and he drifted into a doze, I recalled the tray of engagement rings in the Yiannis' shop and the uncertainty I'd felt at the thought of Kyle slipping one on my finger. Now, though? If he asked me to marry him, I was sure that would be a whole new story.

Sign up for our newsletter and find out about all our romance book releases, eBook sales and promotions, sneak peeks and FREE romance books!

Want to see more from this author? Here's a taster for you to enjoy!

The Fox Family: Fox on the Run
Elizabeth Coldwell

Excerpt

Kyle

The sky over Southend was dark and overcast—the perfect weather for a solemn day. Out of season, the seafront was quiet. Only a few hardy souls walked their dogs along the beach, and most of the shops and restaurants that would be packed with tourists in the height of summer were now shuttered and dark.

I paid the entrance fee to the pier for both Millie and myself, and we stepped onto the faded wooden planking. The place had changed a lot from how I remembered it as a kid—most of the old pier head structure had been rebuilt after it was destroyed in a fire nearly twenty years ago—but the long, slow stroll to the end was still the same.

Millie didn't say a word as we walked, but she took my hand and clutched it tightly. I'd been surprised, and more than a little disappointed, when Mum told me she didn't want to be buried in the big cemetery at Manor Park alongside her own mum and dad. I'd had visions of standing by her graveside, chatting to her like I'd done so often when she'd been alive. Asking for her advice, even though she was no longer around to give it to me. But she'd told me she thought cemeteries were morbid, and even though she'd laid a wreath on her parents' grave every Christmas, she'd always hated those visits. Instead, she wanted me to scatter her ashes in a place that held only happy memories.

"So, you used to come here a lot?" Millie asked as we stood looking down at the lacy froth of the waves around the pillars holding the pier in place.

"Yeah, we'd have day trips every summer when I was little. I used to love it. We'd make sandcastles on the beach, eat ice cream." My face creased in a smile as the memories flooded back. "Sometimes we'd walk out to the end of the pier, then ride back to the seafront on the little train they have. And as I got older, I thought, one day I'll have kids of my own, and I'll bring them here. Maybe their nan will come too…" My voice cracked.

No chance of that happening now, not with Mum gone.

Millie squeezed my hand, offering me silent comfort. She'd been my rock in the days following Mum's death, when I'd been so numb with grief I could barely get out of bed. I'd kept telling myself it wouldn't come as a shock when she passed, given how long I'd had to get used to the knowledge her cancer was terminal. Still, as I'd sat beside Mum's bed in the hospice and she'd taken her final rattling breaths, my first instinct had been to grab the doctor and tell him to do something — anything — to bring her back to me.

"You're doing the right thing, you know, Kyle." Millie leaned a little closer to me. "This is a nice way to say goodbye to her."

As I reached for the straps of my rucksack and shrugged it off my shoulders, light drops of rain began to fall, dampening any urge I might have had to string this moment out. I unzipped the pack and took out the nondescript metal urn containing Mum's ashes.

Her funeral ceremony replayed in my head as I removed the lid of the urn. It had been so different from the previous one I'd attended, only a few months earlier. Charlie Fox's death had attracted hundreds of mourners and a scrum of journalists keen to capture every detail. Only a handful of people had come to say their goodbyes to Mum. It had warmed my heart that Marcia, the nurse who'd done everything she could to keep Mum's spirits up towards the end, had been one of them. The vicar had said a few platitudes, we'd sung *The Lord's My Shepherd*, then Mum's coffin had disappeared behind the crematorium curtain to the strains of *Call Me*, her favourite Blondie song. I pictured her dancing around the kitchen and singing along to it, her voice loud and out of tune, and knew the memory would always keep her alive in my heart.

Millie gave my arm a gentle tap. "Hey, are you okay? Only…" As she spoke, she pulled the hood of her jacket up. The rain was coming harder now, darkening the wooden planks beneath our feet and pelting the surface of the water.

I nodded and took a deep breath. "Goodbye, Mum." My words were barely above a whisper. "Love you." I shook the urn, and the cold grey ashes swirled in the wind as they were carried out to sea.

For a moment after the last of them was gone, I stood staring out over the churning waves. My face was wet, tears mingling with the rainwater, and I swiped at my cheeks. There were so many things I'd never be able to say to Mum now, so many mistakes I'd made that I'd never have the chance to put right. But I couldn't regret the things I'd done, or the life I'd led, because if I'd made different choices, I knew I wouldn't be standing here with Millie by my side.

I turned away from the sea and placed the urn back in the rucksack. I glanced at Millie, who stood lost in her own thoughts. "Come on, let's go a hot drink. I don't know about you, but I'm freezing."

* * * *

We found a little café on the esplanade and grabbed a table next to a couple of men in hi-vis gear who were tucking into full English breakfasts and leafing through newspapers. My stomach growled at the smell of fried food and tomato ketchup, and when the waitress came to take our order, I asked for a bacon and egg sandwich to go with my mug of tea.

When the food arrived, I attacked it as if I hadn't eaten anything for a week.

Millie raised an eyebrow as I wiped egg yolk from my lips.

"What?" I said in answer to her unspoken question. "I couldn't face breakfast this morning. Not when—"

"Hey, I'm not judging you." She laid a hand on my arm. Her gaze was soft and compassionate. "I understand how stressful this must have been. I'll admit, it's making me think about what might happen when my own parents—" She sipped her latte, unable to finish whatever she'd wanted to say.

"It's not just that. The post came before I left the flat. I—I got the sealed deed this morning." She regarded me with a baffled expression, and I went on, "It means they've officially accepted my change of name. I'm Kyle Ferguson-Fox now."

Millie sat back in her seat and fiddled with the end of her ponytail, clearly processing all the implications of my announcement. "You didn't tell me you were planning to do this."

"Well, I've been thinking about it for a while, even before Mum died. When I helped Cameron and Connor rob the jeweller's…that was when I felt like they'd finally accepted me as part of the family. That I was really a brother to them. And it seemed right to combine who'd I always been with who I am now, if that makes sense. So, I downloaded all the forms, went to see a solicitor, did everything by the book." Millie scoffed and I glanced at her. "What's so funny?"

"Just the thought of you complying with the law for once."

"Joke all you want. I can do the right thing when I have to. If I hadn't, you wouldn't be the owner of a successful café right now." I took another bite of my sandwich and chewed as the reality of my new identity continued to sink in. "I was intending to tell you about the deed poll when the time was right. Now I've got to go through the tedious parts of changing all my details with the bank, applying for a new passport, but that should all be easy enough, right? I mean, women do it all the time when they get married, don't they?"

Millie shrugged and set her empty coffee cup down. "That depends on the woman. When my friend Amanda tied the knot, she did the American thing of keeping her maiden name as well as taking her husband's name, even though they got married over here. And as far as I know she didn't have any problems updating her ID, so I doubt you will either."

The two men on the neighbouring table got up to leave. One of them went over to the counter to pay for their breakfasts while the other lingered by the door, scrolling through something on his phone. When I checked my watch, I realised it was almost midday. Glancing out of the window, I noticed the rain appeared to be easing. It was time to head back to

London. I intended to drop Millie off at the café, then spend a quiet afternoon lazing around the flat.

As we got up from the table, my phone rang. I would have let it go to voicemail and deal with whoever was calling when I was home, but the name on the screen demanded immediate attention. It was one of the last people I wanted to speak to, but someone I'd learned better than to ignore.

Henk Brouwer.

About the Author

Elizabeth Coldwell is a multi-published author and editor whose stories have appeared in a number of best-selling anthologies. She has written novels in a variety of different genres, from paranormal to BDSM and contemporary romance. She is the former editor of the UK edition of Forum magazine and the proud winner of an International Leather Award. When she is not busy writing, she is an avid supporter of Rotherham United Football Club and can be regularly found on the terraces at weekends, cheering her boys to victory (hopefully!).

Elizabeth loves to hear from readers. You can find her contact information, website details and author profile page at https://www.firstforromance.com

ENTWINED PUBLISHING

www.ingramcontent.com/pod-product-compliance
Lightning Source LLC
Chambersburg PA
CBHW050533260626
47157CB00004B/1581